FM For Murder

A Pamela Barnes Acoustic Mystery

by

Patricia Rockwell

This book is fiction. All characters, events, and organizations portrayed in this novel are the product of the author's imagination or are used fictitiously. Any resemblance to actual persons—living or dead—is entirely coincidental.

Copyright © 2011 by Patricia Rockwell

All rights reserved. No parts of this book may be reproduced or transmitted in any form or by any means, electronic or mechanical, including photocopying, recording or by any information storage and retrieval system, without written permission from the author, except for the inclusion of brief quotations in a review.

For information, email **Cozy Cat Press**, cozycatpress@aol.com or visit our website at: www.cozycatpress.com

COZY CAT PRESS

LCCN: 2011901039
ISBN: 978-0-9844795-4-2
Printed in the United States of America

Cover design by Scott Saunders of Design 7 Studio, www.design7studio.com

PUBLISHER'S NOTE: The publisher is not responsible for any adverse reaction to eating any of the dishes created from the recipes contained in this book.

10 9 8 7 6 5 4 3 2 1

Dedicated to Harriette, who loved playing the ukulele, wearing anything red, and was always optimistic and joyous.

Chapter 1

Saturday, shortly before midnight, December 15

"Okay, folks out there in radio land, that was Calliope's Doom with their new song, 'Cursed Bones.' Their newest tune, following closely on the heels of their first big, success—Entrails of Love. This is Black Vulture with the best of death and dying, torture and blood. The most alternative of alternative rock for those of you who have nothing better to do on a Saturday night. Make that Sunday morning now here at KRDN, 933 on your FM radio dial. Just a few minutes after midnight. And for those of you crazy enough to stick with me until 4 a.m. (or should I say, those of you, without anything more interesting to do), I'll be playing a host of your favorite songs from some of the best alternative bands in the country.

For example, there's a new CD I just got in from one of my favorite new bands—Ochre Fugue. As you know, Ochre Fugue recently played locally to a packed crowd at the Blue Poppy in downtown Reardon. That was a gig, wasn't it? Obviously, they have lots of fans here in our little berg. I was lucky enough to get to interview Jake Millet with the band. I know, I know; you're all jealous. Well, eat my liver. Getting to interview bands is one of the perks—one of the very few—of my job here at KRDN. Believe me, I don't work here for the pay (hope the station manager isn't listening).

Ah, shoot! Gotta do a commercial now. This one is for— hmm, let's see—Avery's Auto Repair on South Jackson. Let me try to read this with some energy: 'Hey, guys (and ladies), Avery's will fix your wheels for a fair price'—and let's face it—most of us don't have new cars so we probably need a fix-up more often than not, right? But, 'the Avery brothers have been in Reardon for—ever. Simple, honest, repair work. They don't have a fancy location or building, but they do good work. So, check 'em out.' And I'd add to that--especially you students. I mean, Christmas break's coming up in a week or two and if you're planning on driving home to visit Mommy and Poppy you'd better be sure your wheels will make the trip. And you'd better be sure you arrive wearing clean clothes too; parents like that that sort of thing. So I hear.

Okay, now, as I said before, I'm going to be playing a track from Ochre Fugue's new CD. In just a minute. What are you waiting for, right? I first heard this group in the Big Easy, several years ago. I was makin' the rounds of the clubs and ran across this band at a vampire underground party. What a sound they have. Dark. Scary. Like blood, you know, from the coffin. Makes you cringe all over. The bass player has a great get-up. I'd describe 'em in more appropriate language if it weren't for the FCC breathin' down my neck. You know what I'd like to say, though, don't you? All two of you. Don't expect there's too many fans listening in after midnight on a Saturday—unless you're a real loser. Like me. Still working on your graduate degree after six years. Right?

Anyway, I got the Ochre Fugue disc prepped for you. Let's see, which track should I play? Oh, wait. Just heard a car pull up outside the studio. Looks like I've got a visitor. Well, what do you know! That hardly ever happens this far out in the boonies—especially this late. Well, that'll be su—per! I get bored all alone out here at the studio all night long—deejaying and doing all my own tech work. If any of you guys ever want to drop in and visit—great. Just come on by—if you can find it. Okay, here he comes in the door now. Hey, maybe it's a she—better yet! My lucky night!

Oh, hi! Come on in! I'm Theodore Ballard—Black Vulture to my fans. You a fan of alternative rock? What the? Hey, that's a gun! What do you need a gun for? Why're you pointin' it at me? Wha--? No! No!"

Chapter 2

Earlier that week--Tuesday, December 11

Wisps of thin white hair on a small otherwise bald head were all that was visible, peeking out from under the gold satin spread on the large mahogany four poster bed. The old man tipped his head up slowly and squinted in the darkened room.

"Daniel," he whispered to the young man just entering the quiet bed chamber.

Daniel Bridgewater was not tall. He was clean cut and neatly dressed. His round face was unremarkable except when a warm generous smile lit up his soft blue eyes.

"Father," replied the young man, hurrying closer to the bed and grabbing the old man's hands in his. "You're awake."

"They don't let me sleep," said the old man, "They're either giving me a shot or taking my blood pressure." He slowly patted the young man's hands, gnarled veins showing prominently on his hands and arms.

"I'll speak to Katherine," said the young man. "You need your sleep."

"Forget it," answered his father, "Sleep is a waste of time and I have lots to do."

"Right," said Daniel, laughing gently. "I thought we agreed you were going to let me take care of things and you were going to rest."

"Well?" replied his father, "If you're taking care of things, do I get a report?"

"I just came from the office and this morning I was at the plant," said Daniel. "You'll be happy to know that

Fredericks is ahead of schedule on the new broadloom design."

"Good. What about the state government special order?" The old man squeezed his son's hands.

"Almost finished." Daniel closed his palms protectively around his father's clasped hands. The intensity was there, he noted, but the strength was lacking.

"Hmm," his father snorted, "Maybe there is hope for you yet managing this company."

"Glad to hear you have so much faith in me," said Daniel, smiling warmly. He sat up straight and reached for an empty glass on the night stand. Immediately he rang a small silver bell that sat near the glass. Almost at once a middle aged woman in a nurse's uniform complete with an old-fashioned nurse's hat entered the room.

"You needed me, Mr. Bridgewater?" she asked, remaining standing at the door.

"Yes, Katherine," said Daniel, standing, glass in hand, and walking over and handing the glass to her, "Would you please bring my father a fresh glass of water?"

"Yes, sir," she responded and turned and exited.

"I don't need any more water. I need Scotch."

"Scotch? Sounds like you've taken a turn for the better."

"And I'd be better still if you'd let me have the Scotch."

The nurse returned with a glass of water and handed it to Daniel, then exited the room.

"Let's try this first, okay?" he said, bringing the glass to the bed. Sitting on the side of the bed, he held the glass up to his father's mouth. The old man grabbed the rim with trembling hands and gulped noisily as Daniel slowly poured the liquid into his mouth. His father's mouth was dry, his lips cracked. Daniel could tell from just looking at him that his father's health had not improved in the week he'd been in bed. His talk was bravado. He was having difficulty moving and his hands were shaking. Although his words were the same powerful, autocratic demands that Charles Bridgewater was known for; his voice was different--weak, shaky.

"Father, I wish you'd try to relax," said Daniel, replacing the glass on the night stand, the liquid inside only partially drunk. He placed his hand on his father's shoulder and gently eased him back down in the bed. "I've been managing Bridgewater Carpets for—what?—two years now. I think I know what to do without you in the office every day. And besides, I practically followed you around every day for years before that. If you can't trust me to run things, who can you?"

"Daniel," said his father, pulling the young man's shoulder down closer to his ear. "I'm not just concerned about the company. I'm concerned about you." Daniel could smell a rancid odor in his breath.

"Father," said Daniel, stiffly, removing the hand from his shoulder, "I thought we agreed that I can run my own life."

"You can't!" replied Charles Bridgewater, making a sort of gagging noise, seeming to choke as he tried to express his anger. "You're over thirty. You have no private life because you spend all your time running my company. Lord knows, I'm grateful to have you—particularly now. I don't know what I'd do without you. But, you need to be married, you need to be producing heirs. Good God, the Bridgewaters are one of, if not the most, socially prominent families in this entire area. At the rate you're going, the entire family will die out with you. I was hoping you—"

"Father, one thing at a time," said Daniel, squeezing his father's hand tightly and exhaling loudly. "My main concern right now is you—in you getting better. My second concern is the company. Marriage is way, way down the road."

"It should be right on your path. You should stumble over it," replied Charles, squeezing his son's two hands with his, a twinkle in his eye.

"You were obviously quite the ladies' man in your day, Father," said Daniel, shaking his head and chuckling. "Unfortunately, I didn't inherit any of your charm."

"Hell," said Charles, scowling, "you're charming enough. You're rich, Daniel. That's all that those young women care about. Now, listen. When Harold gets here, I want you to talk to him about this woman he knows in Alton. I forget her name. She has a daughter about your age and the family is very well known in---"

"Father, no!"

"You'd deny your dying father his last wish?"

"You're not dying," replied Daniel.

"I am if I say I am." Charles Bridgewater flung himself backwards dramatically—two inches or so onto the pillow.

"For God's sake, father," said Daniel. "You are the most exasperating person."

"That's why I've been so successful. I know what I want and I go after it. How do you think I got your mother?"

"I never heard this story. You chased after mother?" Daniel stood and paced toward the bay window.

"No, not chased. I just conducted a non-stop full-scale blitz until I totally wore her down and she had to agree to marry me."

"Sounds very romantic." Daniel wandered around to the other side of the bed and stood looking down at his aging father. The thin strands of grey crisscrossing his father's otherwise bald pate did not make Charles Bridgewater look very romantic.

"Believe me, it was." The old man grabbed Daniel's hands.

"You don't have a romantic bone in your body." Daniel smiled wide, his eyes twinkling, and stifled a laugh.

"Maybe not any more. But I did. I did. When she was alive..." The old man leaned back on his large pillow, his small head almost vanishing in the white puffs either side of his head. His eyes drifted upward and he seemed to escape to a different world.

"Father..."

Suddenly, the old man's eyes blinked open, as he glanced up at Daniel, seeming somewhat surprised to see his son in the room. He shook himself as if to gather his strength. Then, speaking with a direct and pointed effort, he pointed a wobbly index finger in his son's face.

"Daniel, you get the name of this girl from Harold. Set up a date. You propose. You marry. Step by step. Think of it just like taking over a small company. Shouldn't take too long. Harold can help with the details of the wedding."

"Thanks, but no thanks, Father. I can do my own romancing and I don't care to consider my love life like a business take-over." He shook his head in amazement that such a sick old man could find the strength to play Yentl.

"Obviously you need help or you'd be married by now. And besides, you're all I have left now..."

"Father, you know that's not true. You have...."

"Quiet. I told you never to talk about.... Never ever." He stared at Daniel, a grim set to his mouth. Suddenly, he waved his hand. "Give me more water." With that, the old man started choking uncontrollably, reaching his arm up, gesturing for water. Daniel ran around to the other side of the bed and grabbed the glass on the night stand. He quickly dripped a steady stream of droplets into the old man's mouth. He felt like a mother bird feeding a chick—a bird that was all mouth and no body. His father was the most stubborn person he knew—the most determined, but the most stubborn. Well, he thought, I'm his son. After a few swallows, the choking subsided. The old man laid back on his pillow, exhausted. Daniel looked at him and shook his head.

"What I want, Father, is for you to get well, and I'm not going to even consider thinking about anything else—except the company of course—until you're up and about and your old self again." He put his hand on the old man's head and traced the thin top hair with his finger. "It's almost Christmas. You love Christmas. You should see the office. Bernice has it decorated beautifully. And over at the plant too. Everyone is concerned about you. They want you well."

"Don't count on it." The old man closed his eyes. Daniel waited a minute to see if it was a ploy or if he was being dismissed. After a few moments, he realized that his father was through with their discussion. He hadn't been able to browbeat him into submission with the strength of his personality—not anymore. Now he was just a sick old man. Daniel was right and he knew it. His father needed to concentrate on getting better—not on managing the business or on his son's personal life. But, Lord, it would be hard for him to give up doing what he'd done for so many years.

Daniel quietly pulled the covers on the bed up under his father's chin again. When he was certain that his father was resting comfortably, he tiptoed out of the bedroom. There he immediately saw Katherine, the nurse, sitting on a nearby chair, reading a magazine. She jumped up when Daniel entered.

"Mr. Bridgewater," she said, "Dr. Knowles would like to speak with you for a moment. He just stepped out but he'll be right back. I'm going back to sit with your father...."

At that moment, a tall middle aged man came down the long hallway of the old mansion. He carried a stethoscope in one hand and a medical bag in the other.

"Mr. Bridgewater," he said to Daniel. The nurse nodded to the two men and slipped into the bedroom.

"Doctor Knowles, I'm glad you were able to stay. I'd like to find out how you think my father is doing. He certainly seemed in better spirits today."

"Mr. Bridgewater," said the doctor. "I'll grant you that. His spirits are remarkable, considering."

"Considering what?"

"Considering that he has very little time left."

Chapter 3

Present time--Sunday Morning, December 16

Pamela Barnes stretched her legs under the warm covers. Her comfy down bedspread was so toasty. She just wanted to enjoy sleeping late and not having to leap out of bed at 6 a.m. and get ready for class. Sunday, the perfect day. Even better, she felt her husband's arm slip around her waist and his rough, whisker-covered cheek rub against the back of her neck. Definitely better.

Suddenly, she heard a series of little yelps and small footsteps pummeling her back and a tiny tongue licking her nose. As she carefully opened one eye, she saw what she knew was happening. Her energetic poodle was not enjoying everyone sleeping late on the weekend and was anxious to get up. Therefore, the entire household had to get up with him.

"Candide!" she scolded, shooing him away from her face. "Down! You know you're not supposed to get on our bed."

"He won't get down until you get up," added her husband Rocky, pulling his pillow over his head and rolling over.

"Me? Why should I get up?" squeaked Pamela, turning on her mate and nudging him in the side. "He's just as much your dog."

"Thanks a lot, Candide," said the large husky man to the small dog. "If men knew how much dogs would get in the way of their sex lives, they'd never own them." He sat up, leaning back on his palms.

"It seems to me that you manage to find plenty of times when Candide is sleeping to..." She pushed her husband back on the bed, bent over to his ear and whispered something. Candide jumped on Rocky's stomach and proceeded to jump up and down. The little white dog accompanied his antics with additional barking.

"All right, all right," said Rocky, sitting back up, picking the small white dog up in his massive hands and placing him gently on the floor beside the bed. "You made your case, buddy. We're getting up." He flung back the covers and swung his large feet to the ground. Standing, he grabbed a pair of worn jeans from the back of a chair and stepped into them. "You getting up?" he asked, turning to his wife.

"Could I stay here?" she ventured, leaning back on the headboard. "I promise to keep your place warm for you."

"Thanks." He scowled at her and trudged around the bed, stopping to bend and kiss her forehead. "Now that I'm up, I guess I'll make pancakes."

"Umm," she replied, closing her eyes and smiling. "Sounds heavenly. Here Candide, come to Mommy." She reached out a hand over the edge of the bed and gestured for the little dog to come to her.

"Pam," said her husband, "you know he won't stay here if he sees me heading for the kitchen."

Before Rocky had disappeared from the bedroom, Pamela called out to him. "Do you know what time Angie got in last night? Did you hear her? I must have fallen asleep."

He stopped at the doorway, turned and said, "Late. I was in bed, but I heard her come in around 1 a.m."

"That's good."

"Good? That's later than I think she should get home. Don't you think?"

"Rocky, she's in college. If she'd gone away to school, she'd probably be staying out all night."

"Not if I had anything to say about it." He headed off around the corner, followed by Candide, and into the kitchen where Pamela soon heard doors and drawers slamming open and shut, and pots and pans crashing. Being a father of a girl, she thought, was obviously much harder on Rocky than it was on her. Their only child, Angela, was now a sophomore in college and lived at home while she studied at the local college, Grace University, where both Pamela and Rocky taught. As their child, Angela received reduced tuition which helped greatly with expenses. Small town college teachers did not make huge salaries.

"She's a good girl," Pamela shouted at him from the bedroom. All she heard in return were mumbles and grunts. Time to get out of bed, she said to herself, whether I want to or not. She reluctantly shoved back the covers and plopped her feet over the edge and into her waiting slippers. Grabbing her robe from her nearby armchair, she wrapped it around herself as she headed for the kitchen to provide assistance. She realized that it would probably only be moral support because her kitchen skills were nominal at best. Rocky was the kitchen guru in the family. In fact, he was probably the best chef in the neighborhood having perfected his craft throughout his twenty years as an Army cook.

"Hey," she said, smiling at him as she entered their spotless, gleaming kitchen—the only room in the house that could claim that honor. Rocky was proud of his work—and his workplace. The rest of the house was her domain and as long as she didn't trip over any clutter, it was clean enough for her. "Can I help?"

"Unlikely," he snorted.

"You're mad at me?" she asked, pouting sweetly. "I'm sorry about Candide waking us up."

"Nah, I'm just remembering about Angie getting in so late. I'm not sure I like this business of her growing up."

"No father does."

"Or that hoodlum she's dating…."

"Rocky, that hoodlum is my graduate assistant, Kent. He's a very conscientious young man."

"Yeah, I know," responded her husband. "But he looks like a weirdo. What's with his hair anyway?"

"I don't know. It's how lots of them wear it. Some kind of strange gel."

"It's purple."

"Well, there's that too." She shrugged.

During this conversation, Rocky had set out the ingredients for his special homemade pancakes. He now had the thin batter prepared and the griddle heated and sizzling.

Candide was waiting patiently and quietly by his feet, in anticipation of receiving some sort of edible treat.

"Here," he called to his wife, "you can flip these when they're ready." He motioned her to the stove and handed her a spatula.

"Rocky, I don't know," she replied, pulling her hand back hesitantly. "I'm not very good at frying things. You know what happened the last time."

"Yeah, Mom, you almost burned the house down," interjected their daughter Angela, who had appeared at the kitchen doorway, wrapped in a small bedspread, her long auburn hair, hanging in her face, her eyes barely open. She yawned.

"Sorry, Angie," said Pamela, turning towards her daughter. "Did we wake you?"

"No, I smelled Dad's pancakes," replied Angie and scooted her bedspread-clad body towards the stove where she reached her hand out and grabbed the spatula from her father. "I can flip, Dad. Better eye-hand coordination than Mom." She yawned again and leaned against the counter. Candide scrunched up close to his young mistress, hiding within the folds of her bedspread, his face skyward towards the griddle.

"Did you have a nice time last night?" asked Pamela, sitting down on a kitchen stool.

"Yeah, fine," responded Angela, focusing on the griddle.

"What time did you get in?" asked Rocky, stirring the mixture, and adding cinnamon and nutmeg.

"After midnight," answered Angela. "Oh, and Mom, a weird thing happened." Rocky paused scooping cupfuls of the mixture onto the griddle.

"Weird?" asked Rocky, "Weird how?" He peered at his daughter with a worried frown.

"On the radio," said Angela. "Kent and I were at Pookie's after the movie. We were just sitting there having slushies and listening to KRDN—this show that plays alternative music on Saturday night. The deejay was talking and introducing songs and stuff and somebody came into the studio and this whoever it was evidently had a gun and we heard a gunshot and then nothing." She carefully flipped pancakes as she spoke.

"What?" bellowed her father. He had now proceeded to whipping up home made syrup and frying bacon.

"You heard a gunshot?" asked Pamela.

"Yeah, that's what it sounded like," said Angela. "We weren't sure. After we heard the shot, there was no more talking. Then it sounded like the mike was turned off and that was it. We didn't know what to think."

"Oh my God," said Pamela, leaning her elbows on the counter. "You must have been shocked."

"You're sure it was a gunshot? Maybe it was part of the music? I mean, some of that music is very strange." Rocky questioned her, as he stirred his special syrup on the burner next to the griddle.

"No, Dad, believe me. It was a gunshot. Besides, the deejay said the person who came into the studio had a gun. I think the person came into the studio with a gun and shot the deejay." Angela was bleary-eyed but still clear-headed enough to report the facts.

"Oh my God," repeated Pamela. "This was a local station?"

"Yeah," answered her daughter, "KRDN, FM 933. I always listen to that show late on Saturday because it has music they don't play on any other station. Kent too." She flipped a little brown circle on the skillet.

"So," said Rocky, continuing to stir his syrup and staring at his daughter, "you heard this shot and then just nothing. Dead air?"

"And maybe a dead deejay," responded Angela. She looked at her parents and shrugged.

"Surely," said Pamela, standing and getting plates and silverware from the cupboards, "someone must have reported this."

"We did," said Angela. "Kent called the station first and all he got was a recording. Then, he called the local police and reported to them that we had heard a shooting on KRDN and the time. Evidently, we weren't the first. They'd already received a few other calls with the same report."

"So," continued Rocky, nodding, "I suppose they must have sent an officer to the studio to check on this deejay to see if he was hurt or if it was a prank or what?" He finished stirring the syrup and turned off the burner under the bacon.

"I guess," answered Angela, flipping the pancakes onto the waiting plates.

"Good thing you didn't call your mother or she'd have gone over there and solved the case with a whisk of her magic spectrograph before dawn. Just like the one she solved last year." He directed his last comment and a pointed glare in Pamela's direction.

Pamela ignored her husband's sarcasm. Her penchant for getting involved in things she had no business getting involved in—such as murder investigations--had caused one of the few rifts in their otherwise happy marriage. As Rocky topped each plate with copious amounts of his syrup, she continued "You know, maybe the station is reporting on it by now. It's..." she looked at the kitchen clock, "nine o'clock. Maybe by now, they know what happened and will be reporting it—at least at KRDN. You said 933 FM?" Angela nodded as Pamela disappeared into the bedroom and quickly returned with a small transistor radio. She set the dial, turned the switch, and placed the radio in the center of the kitchen table. The family slurped up their pancakes and bacon as they listened intently to the local broadcast.

"...so, the police don't have a clue to the identity of the killer..." the announcer was saying.

"Oh my God," Pamela interjected.

Angela sucked in her breath and Rocky froze.

"But from the several calls received by the station last night and by replaying recordings of last night's program, the police believe that the murder took place shortly after midnight—at KRDN—out on Highway 27. As I've been reporting, KRDN disc jockey, Theodore Ballard, known as The Black Vulture, host of our late Saturday night alternative rock program was shot and killed last night while he was on air. An unknown person entered the studio and shot him and then disappeared. Several listeners reported hearing the event as it occurred and immediately called the police.

When the police arrived at the studio, they found Ballard's body on the floor beside his microphone—shot in the head. Our station manager Roger Gallagher will be updating our listeners as he receives information from the police. In the mean time, KRDN will continue broadcasting its regular programming from our mobile unit until the police allow us back into the studio."

With that, Pamela switched off the radio and the three of them looked at each other with total surprise.

"Somebody just walked into a radio station and shot this guy?" pondered Rocky, shaking his head.

"Yeah," said Angela, "KRDN is really isolated, Dad. It's way out on the outskirts of town."

"And he was all alone?" asked Pamela.

"Evidently," responded his daughter.

"Wait a minute," said Rocky, holding up his hand, "His name is Theodore Ballard—Ted Ballard?"

"Yeah," said Angela, "he really knows alt music. Kent says he's the best around here. Nobody knows Goth like The Black Vulture."

"I know this guy," said Rocky, his fork slowing on its way to his mouth.

"How?" asked Pamela, her face a canvas of concern.

"He's one of our doctoral students—in the English department. I think Trudi's his advisor."

"Trudi Muldoon?" asked his wife.

"Yes," Rocky replied. "I didn't really know him, but I've seen him in her office—and of course he taught freshman comp—just like a lot of us. God, it makes me feel like I know him. He probably walked by my office door every day and I never even said 'hello.' God, how horrible." He set his fork down on his plate.

"Horrible," seemed the perfect cue for the telephone to ring—which it did.

"Hello," answered Rocky, as he reached over and grabbed the receiver from the wall phone in the small kitchen. "Yeah, hi. We were just talking about you. Yeah, we just heard. My God, awful. They're questioning you? Why? Awful. Yeah. Yeah." Rocky listened patiently to the voice on the phone as Pamela waited impatiently and attempted to determine the gist of the conversation from her end. Angela seemed lost in her pancakes. When Rocky hung up, he looked stung.

"That was Trudi," he said to the two women. "She's at the office. The police are there going through Ted's office. They've questioned her a bit, but they're planning on re-questioning her when they finish in Ted's office. They told her to stay there and not go anywhere. She wants me to come down there and wait with her."

"I don't mind if you go, Rocky," said Pamela, clutching her husband's arm tightly. "If that will help her, go. I know you and Trudi are friends."

"That's not all," he added, looking pointedly at Pamela, "she wants you to come down too."

"Me?"

"Yeah," he said, "because of all your experience working with the police." He said this last part between clenched teeth. "You're the murder expert in the family, you know."

Chapter 4

Previous week--Tuesday, December 11

Daniel Bridgewater sat in his office on the second floor at the Bridgewater Carpet Company's office building. He was at his large marble-topped desk but he was turned away, facing out a large bay window that overlooked the Bridgewater manufacturing plant across from the office parking lot and the circular entrance drive which surrounded it, the beautiful Bridgewater fountain still busily pumping water even though the December temperatures were hovering in the 40's. It was good that the weather never really got cold enough this far south to freeze the water, thought Daniel. His father Charles had built the fountain for his mother years ago in memory of their honeymoon, and it was one of Daniel's favorite parts of the office compound—an otherwise bland and stuffy structure.

He clutched his coffee cup and held it to his lips even though he had finished the brew inside hours ago. He was trying to make sense of conflicting signals. His father had seemed so much better this morning—more talkative, more cheerful. Yet, when he had spoken to his father's personal physician, Dr. Knowles, the prognosis seemed even bleaker than they had previously thought. Charles Bridgewater, 76, founder and head of Bridgewater Carpets, was suffering from congestive heart failure. Had been for quite a while. He'd been on numerous different medications which had seemed to be working—at least they had to Daniel. His father was in the office daily, and although Daniel had officially taken over the reins of the company several years ago, Charles still kept his hand in the pot and that was fine with Daniel. He enjoyed his father's company and their regular sparring. Daniel was still learning the in's and out's of the carpet business—he probably would still be learning for years—the carpet manufacturing business was a world unto itself—at least in the United States. Most of it was centered in Dalton, Georgia, but several large companies—such as Bridgewater--had set up shop in neighboring states and were actually successful.

How could his father seem so much better when Dr. Knowles seemed to think he was getting worse? And that was exactly what Knowles had said to Daniel when he left his father's bedroom earlier in the morning. Tests showed that his heart capacity was declining. When Daniel mentioned this discrepancy to the doctor, the physician had replied that Charles was probably struggling to appear normal. Lord, thought Daniel, I don't want him to overexert himself just to pretend to me that he's feeling better. But what could he do about it? Daniel tipped his desk chair back and forth as he followed the bursts of water from the fountain. The three cupids in the center each held curved horns and the water jets shot from each in beautiful curves. The fountain was based on a fountain in Italy that Daniel's mother had fallen in love with when she and Charles had gone there on their honeymoon. When Elinore had died 12 years ago in a car accident, the fountain had taken on even greater meaning. Now, it appeared Charles would follow his beloved wife in death. At least, according to Knowles, his father didn't have much time left. How much time, Knowles wasn't willing to say. Daniel knew he should be doing something constructive, but right now he was frozen with indecision. His father was dying. He didn't know how long he had; it might be only a few weeks—even days. He wasn't really worried about the business, because Bridgewater Carpets was doing well—even in the present poor economy. People still needed carpeting, at least enough people did. Theirs was a fairly stable business. Daniel had learned the ropes well and he had a support staff that helped him run the place so that he could concentrate on catering to his father at this difficult time. No one would miss him if he spent much or even all of his time at home by his father's bedside.

No, the business wasn't his main worry now. That wasn't what was causing Daniel to gnaw on the edge of his coffee cup and stare morosely out at the fountain in the circle. No. I probably should just go back and sit by his bedside, he thought. Forget anything else. Just let well enough alone. Why stir up a hornet's nest? He turned his desk chair around and placed his coffee cup back on his desk. He picked up a large maroon and gold embossed photograph album that was lying on the left side of his desk. The album was thick and photographs were sticking out from the crinkled pages inside. Daniel placed the album in front of him and opened the cover. He slowly turned to the first page.

A buzz sounded from the intercom to his right.

"Yes, Bernice?"

"Mr. Bridgewater, Mr. Vickers is here to see you."

"Fine. Send him in." Drumming his fingers on the first page of the album, Daniel closed the cover and placed the large book to his left.

"Daniel," said a gray-haired man entering, "Bernice told me about Charles." He grabbed Daniel's hand in half shake and half embrace. Daniel motioned for him to be seated in one of the two green leather chairs situated in front of his desk.

"I don't understand it, Harold," said Daniel to the man, "he seemed better to me this morning. Yet, Knowles said his heart is getting worse."

"If I know your father, Daniel," replied Vickers, "he'll fight to the end. He'd never want anyone to think he was hurting." Vickers leaned back in his chair and unbuttoned his suit coat. The lawyer looked at home and well he should as he had served the position of family and company attorney since Charles had founded the business.

"You think that's it?"

"I think he's a fighter. I think he'll hold on as long as he can."

"I wish I knew how long that was," said Daniel, forming a tent of his fingers and leaning his chin on them.

"Just enjoy being with him—and let him enjoy you for as long as you've got," said Vickers, gesturing and sighing audibly. Vickers' grey hair was worn slicked back. He looked elegant, but his manner was down to earth.

"That's not enough."

"What more can you do?"

"You know."

"God, you aren't contemplating that fool idea again, are you?" Vickers' chiseled features reddened.

Daniel scowled at the man; he picked up the album and flipped through the first five or six pages, stopping at a page and focusing his attention on a small photograph on the left page.

"This is the last picture we have of him."

"So?"

"So, I want to find him."

"Why now?"

"Because..." Daniel stared at the small photograph, seemingly lost in thought.

"Because your father is dying?" Vickers asked. When Daniel failed to respond, Vickers stood and grabbed the album from his hands, closing it at the same time.

"We went through this years ago, Daniel. You wanted to find him and I explained to you that your father did not want him found. David doesn't want to be found. You're the only one who seems to care where he is. Why would you bring this up now?"

"Because Father has a right to see David before he dies." Daniel rose and slammed his palms on his desk. Vickers strode around the office, speaking as if he were addressing a jury.

"Right? What right? He doesn't care; he's not interested. You're the only one who's ever been at all concerned about what happened to David. David has shown no interest in contacting you. Maybe he's not even alive. Have you ever thought of that?"

"Yes, which makes it even more important that I find him. They call it closure, Harold. My father needs to know and he needs to know soon." Daniel remained standing at the desk, staring at the attorney.

"I think you're totally misreading what will and what will not make your father's death easier for him."

"I'm his son. I ought to know." Vickers crossed to Daniel and put his hands of the young man's shoulders. "Yes, but I'm his lawyer; I've known him longer than you have. Charles Bridgewater is not sentimental—with the exception, of course, for Elinore. That I never did figure out. As far as business goes, he's as ruthless as they come. He will die peacefully because he knows he's leaving the company in good hands—your hands. That's all you need to worry about. Take care of the company and you'll make your father's last days happy. Don't try to pull some crazy stunt that will just lead to heartbreak for him—and probably for you." He walked back to the green leather chair in front of Daniel's desk and sat.

"It's not a crazy stunt. Listen, Harold. I'm determined to do this whether you like it or not," said Daniel, walking around his desk and sitting on the edge, where he spoke to Vickers in close face-to-face contact. "Knowles says Father doesn't have long. I'd leave now and go out on my own to track him down, but I really feel I need to stay here and be close to Dad. I know you know people who can help me with this—who can investigate this discreetly. I'd appreciate you putting me in contact with one of them. Will you? Or will I have to go track down some fly-by-night PI on my own from the Yellow Pages?" He leaned over Vickers and stared until Vickers literally blinked.

"Okay, okay, Daniel," replied Vickers, breaking eye contact and forcing Daniel to stand and return to his desk chair. "If you are determined to pursue this little project, I'll find you someone responsible and reliable." He rubbed his palms together, shaking his head, "but I think this is extremely unwise. I want to go on the record."

"Consider it recorded, Harold," replied Daniel, sitting in his desk chair. "Just send me an investigator I can trust. Now, have you seen Father today?"

"I have. I just came from the house."

"And?"

"I agree with the doctor," replied Vickers, crossing his legs and leaning back in the chair. "He seemed in the worst shape I've seen him in ages." His voice softened and he was noticeably pained to say this last item.

"That bad?" Daniel slumped in his chair as he fixed his eyes on the man across from him.

"Yes. I think he's presenting you his best face."

"I don't want that."

"Consider it one of the obligations of parenthood." Vickers set his jaw. Daniel was like a son.

Daniel bent over his desk, head in hands. "What can I do to get him to relax?"

"Daniel, I think if he relaxes, he's gone. Let him have this—this desire to impress you. It's keeping him alive. Oh, and a plan to get you married off to Margaret Millwood's daughter." He crossed his arms and gave Daniel a sideways smirk.

Daniel looked over his shoulder. "Oh, no, not that again." Then, looking directly at Vickers and then sideways at the album, he said, "Forget that. Just get me that investigator and quick."

Vickers started to say something, then nodded, and exited without a word. Daniel remained seated, head in hands. He reached into his suit jacket pocket and brought out his iPhone. Quickly he tapped in a number.

"Hi, Sweet, how are you?" He listened for the answer which caused him to smile warmly. "He seemed better to me, but the doctor said he's worse. Knowles says he doesn't have much time left.... I don't know....Father? He was very talkative ... giving orders...running my life—just like normal. He's planning to marry me off to some society woman's daughter he knows. No? I thought you'd laugh at that."

While he listened in response to his call, Daniel leaned back in his chair and put his feet on his desk. He rocked the chair back and forth rhythmically as he responded with frequent "um's" and "yes's." The intensity of the recent discussion with the lawyer had morphed into a gentle, chat.

"Vickers was just here. He thinks Father is doing worse. I'm afraid I believe him. I have to believe what the doctor says. Anyway, I'm having Vickers get me an investigator—to find David. I know. It's probably a hopeless cause, but I need to find him before Father dies."

Chapter 5

Present --Sunday afternoon, December 16

Silverton Hall was one of the tallest buildings on the Grace University campus, five stories. Rocky's office was on the top floor. Just two buildings away from Pamela's Blake Hall, home of the Psychology Department, Silverton housed the much larger English and Foreign Language Departments. As Pamela followed her husband in the side entrance, she found herself huffing to keep up with her mate.

"Slow down, Rocky," she panted.

"What's the matter?" he asked, not missing a beat as he peered over his shoulder at her. "I thought you'd been working out at your gym. Weren't you bragging the other day about the number of reps you could do or something?" He rounded the corner and entered the stairwell. The old building echoed. It was obviously quite deserted on a Sunday afternoon.

"I am. I can," she replied, following him as he easily took two steps at a time. "Jeez, Rocky! It's not a contest."

"Okay, okay," he answered, sighing and slowing noticeably as he backtracked and took her elbow in mock concern. "Do you need help, Grandma?" Pamela snatched her arm from him, annoyed. It was evident how Rocky stayed in shape even while eating his own marvelous cooking. If she had to trudge up and down five flights of stairs every day, she'd be in great form too.

"Isn't there an elevator in Silverton?" she asked, snarling and looking at him sideways.

"Sure," he responded, "at the other end of the building. I never use it."

"So I can tell." She traipsed ever slower as they finally rounded the last landing before the final floor. She could see the hallway and the office doors ahead. She had been to Rocky's office only a few times—as he had to hers. Their home was neutral ground, but she was well aware of much of what went on in the English Department as they enjoyed sharing tales of woe (and triumph) about their own academic areas.

The couple walked about halfway down the main hallway and then turned down a long barren side hallway with a sign indicating "Faculty Offices, 520-530." Rocky's office was directly across the hall from Trudi Muldoon's. Trudi was an Associate Professor and technically outranked Rocky, but the two were about the same age and had similar outlooks on life, so they frequently found themselves standing outside their office doors chatting.

When Pamela and Rocky arrived at Trudi's office, they could tell she was inside because her door was open and light spilled out into the hall. Rocky walked to the doorway and peeked inside. Pam remained behind him.

Trudi Muldoon sat at her desk in the corner of the windowless room. Pamela noticed that Trudi had not decorated her office with much of anything except many bookshelves. There were several wooden chairs with arm rests stationed in front of Trudi's desk. When she saw the couple in the door, Trudi immediately stood.

"Rocky, Pam, come in," she said, coming from behind her desk and ushering them in. Trudi was a tall woman, flat-chested with a plain but friendly face. Her buck teeth were her most obvious feature along with a mop of flyaway brown hair. Her slightly oversized flowered dress did not coordinate at all well with her Oxford loafers.

Rocky and Pamela entered, removed their winter jackets, and sat in the chairs in front of the desk. Trudi returned to the desk. "I wish I had something to offer you to drink. This all happened so fast and I've been sitting here waiting for them to finish and come back. Oh my God, I'm just a wreck."

"Where are they now?" asked Rocky, "The Police?"

"I guess down in Ted's office. It's on the fourth floor," she said.

"Trudi," began Pamela, "why did you get dragged down here anyway?"

"Didn't Rocky tell you?" said Trudi, "Ted was my doctoral advisee. I was his supervisor too. Actually, I was here working on a project when they showed up. Dr. Marbury told them I'd probably be here. They asked me just a few questions—I guess to make sure I knew Ted and then they went off to examine his office. They told me to stay here and they'd be back to ask me more questions."

"How long have you been waiting?" asked Pamela.

"I don't know, maybe an hour or more," replied the woman behind the desk. She drew her hands to her chin and leaned her elbows on the desk. "Pam, I know you went through this last year—when you found Charlotte in your lab. Rocky told me all about it. I figured you'd understand what I'm feeling. I didn't find Ted or see his body—like you did. But Ted's my student—so we were quite close. Doctoral students become so tied to us. Like children. I just can't believe this has happened." She put her hands to her head and rubbed her temples as if doing so would relieve her distress.

"Do you want me to go down there and see what's happening?" asked Rocky.

"No," Trudi responded. "Just wait with me, will you?"

"Of course, we will," responded Pamela, as she reached over the desk and grabbed Trudi's hand, the one she had just lowered from her face.

"Trudi," began Rocky, "do you have any knowledge that you think will help the police find Ted's killer? I mean, did he have any enemies?"

"Enemies?" asked Trudi, her eyes widening, her buck teeth protruding.

"Surely, this wasn't just a random killing," added Pamela, "I understand someone actually shot him while he was on the radio."

"You've heard about it, then?" asked Trudi. She grabbed a tissue from a box on her desk and patted her eyes.

"Actually," said Rocky, "our daughter and her boyfriend were listening to KRDN at the time it happened. They didn't know if it was real or a hoax. Our daughter told us about it this morning and then we turned on the radio and KRDN was reporting about the shooting on their news report."

"Oh, my God," said Trudi, "It's just awful. I can't imagine why anyone would do this. I just can't imagine." She poked the tissue around the corner of each eye.

"So, he didn't have any enemies?" asked Pamela.

"Pam, what enemies would he have? He was just a doctoral student in English. Really, he was kind of a loner—kind of kept to himself. But, a pleasant enough fellow. He was on assistantship." One of Trudi's large front teeth bit down over her lower lip.

"A teaching assistantship?" asked Pamela.

"That's about the only kind we have in English," Trudi replied. "He taught several sections of Freshman Comp—just like you Rocky."

"Maybe an irate student did this. Maybe it was some student he failed," suggested Pamela.

"Maybe," said Trudi, nodding, her tousled hair flopping back and forth, "He spent most of his time working on his dissertation. He was ABD."

"All but dissertation. So, he was about done then," said Rocky.

"Well," said Trudi, hesitating. "I wish that were true." Her two large front teeth took turns gnawing on her lip.

"What do you mean?" asked Pamela.

"Oh, Pam, Rocky," replied the tall woman, "I wish I could say he was close to finishing but he was struggling. I had high hopes for him originally. He breezed through his Master's thesis with me. He's a good writer and researcher. But somehow, he got started on this dissertation and it just wasn't working out…"

"How so?" asked Rocky.

"He was doing an analytical study of the musicality in the poetry of Edgar Allen Poe—a very clever idea. It was a nice interdisciplinary effort. He had two committee members from the Music Department in addition to me and Dr. Allen and Dr. Hitchcock from our Department. Then, all of a sudden, a few months ago, he decided to trash this study that was—for all intents and purposes—finished, and start completely over with a creative dissertation."

"And by 'creative' you mean..." said Rocky.

"I mean he intended to write his own creative work," she replied, "a gothic novel in the style of Poe. Or more rightly, in the style of this modern 'Goth' trend that seems to be everywhere—in the literature, music, dress—everywhere in modern culture." She sighed and shook her head.

"Did you approve of this change?" asked Pamela.

"Of course not," replied Trudi. "I told him it was foolish but he was insistent. He even produced several drafts. I went over the first draft and immediately sent it back to him with major criticisms. I told him—begged him--to return to his previous research topic. I warned him that he was jeopardizing his assistantship by making such a huge change in his dissertation so late in the process. Did he consider his committee? Did he realize that his assistantship couldn't continue forever? Did he realize that starting from scratch would mean adding months if not years to his completion time? I made all these arguments, believe me."

"And still he insisted on writing this creative project," said Rocky, with a hint of disdain.

"Yes," she replied, "and it seemed to take over his life. He started to change the way he dressed, his hair, everything. I mean, before, he was just a normal looking graduate student--if such an animal exists—jeans, sneakers, t-shirt. Then he started this Goth novel thing, and he began to morph into his characters I guess. Heavy boots, long black pants and shirts. He wore this long black trench coat everywhere. And weird, scary designs all over it—like dragons and bats. His hair was a mess; he never combed it and—oh my god—eye liner. I know I've seen some males do that, but, believe me when a male you know all of a sudden shows up wearing it—it's a shock."

"I know," said Pamela, "my graduate assistant dresses somewhat in that style. But he's incredibly conscientious. It doesn't seem to affect his work ethic."

Rocky gave his wife a sideways glance.

"The ultimate question, though, I guess," said Rocky, "is what was the likelihood that he would have finished this creative work and earned his dissertation?"

"I'll let you decide," replied Trudi, opening a drawer in her desk, removing a folder, and selecting a small stapled typed manuscript from inside. "Here." She handed the article to Rocky. Pamela leaned close to her husband and looked over his shoulder as he read a paragraph from the paper aloud:

> "Swirling,
> Whirling
> The bloody vortex pulls me down
> Down to the eternal abyss
> Overhead
> The black vultures of death circle
> Watching
> Waiting
> To pick the flesh from my dissipated body
> Only my soul remains
> And that you have killed
> With your loveless eyes"

Rocky put the paper on Trudi's desk and shook his head.

"Is that good poetry?" asked Pamela.

"Not by my standards," answered Trudi, "and unfortunately not by the standards of members of his committee. I tried to tell him that. He said he'd improve it. He did do some rewrites. But, Rocky, Pam, nothing really improved. This is about the best of it. And it's generally awful. Just garbage. Six years. Six years of this young man's life and all he had to show for it was this."

"You couldn't talk him into going back to the other project?" asked Pamela.

"I tried, Pam, but he was adamant. I had about reached the end of my ideas. I was going to have to tell him that I couldn't approve his new dissertation proposal and that we were going to drop his assistantship—and he knew it."

"No more funding," said Pamela.

"Right," said Trudi, "and once that happened, all he'd have to live on, as far as I know, would be that deejay job which is only four hours on Saturday. He couldn't make much money from that."

"So, in a way, his murder solves the problem of funding," said Rocky, looking at both women.

"What would he have done without his assistantship?" asked Pamela. "Did he have family that would support him?"

"As far as I know, there was no one. He was a loner. He never spoke about a family. He was very closed mouthed about his private life. I guess though, that the police will find out about that. Won't they?"

At that moment, a large man wearing a grey overcoat appeared in the door, followed by a uniformed police officer.

"The police will find out about what?" he asked the threesome sitting in the small office.

"Oh, Detective," said Trudi, standing, "we were just wondering about Ted's family. I don't know if he had any relatives. This is my colleague Rocky Barnes and his wife—Pamela. This is the detective in charge of the investigation of Ted's murder. Detective Shoop."

"Dr. Barnes and I have met," said the tall man, entering a few steps into the office, eyeing Pamela with a frown, "We spent quite a bit of time together following the death of Charlotte Clark in the Psychology Department last year. Didn't we? I'm delighted to finally meet your husband, Doctor." He turned to Rocky and shook his hand. "You have my sympathies, Mr. Barnes," he whispered as he bent towards Rocky.

Chapter 6

Previous week--Tuesday afternoon, December 11

Daniel Bridgewater sat in a back booth at Sam's Diner, a small eatery on the highway near the entrance to his carpet factory. His coffee cup was half-full and he was gazing at the photo that he had removed earlier from the album in his office. He hardly noticed when one of the waitresses popped up beside him, coffee pot in hand.

"Refill, Mr. Bridgewater?"

"Sure, warm 'er up," he replied, smiling at the young woman whose name tag proclaimed her as "Amy." "Then have a seat."

"No can do, Mr. B," replied the waitress, her pony tail flipping jauntily as she spoke. "Some of us have to work for a living."

Daniel peeked around the corner of the booth. He was the only customer in the small restaurant. A cashier sat at the entrance, totally engrossed in filing her nails. "Doesn't look all that busy to me," he said, smiling as he grabbed her wrist and gently tried to pull her into the booth.

"Just a minute," whispered Amy, and as quickly as she had appeared, she disappeared. Within another second, she had returned and slid into the booth across from Daniel. "Had to get rid of the coffee pot. Okay, I'm seated. What's up?"

"I just like to see your beautiful face," he said, taking her hands and pulling her across the booth where he planted a quick kiss on her lips.

"Dan," said Amy, "please, someone may be watching." She pulled away and slid far back into the bench of her side of the booth.

"So what?"

"If you remember, all this secrecy was your idea," replied Amy, brushing some crumbs off of her otherwise spotless chiffon apron. Her eyes danced with a lively energy. "I'm not ashamed of you."

"And I'm not ashamed of you!" he exclaimed. "I'm trying to figure out how to handle everything that's going on." He bent over the table and spoke confidentially. "A lot is going on, you know."

"I know. I heard what you said on the phone." Amy crossed her arms and glared at Daniel. "You really are in a pickle, aren't you? What's that?" she asked, pointing to the photo that Daniel was fingering.

"It's David," he replied, turning the picture around and holding it up for Amy to see. "High school graduation."

"It's him?" she asked, taking the picture from Daniel.

He nodded. "Yeah, he graduated from Dexter Military Academy. Blue and gold were their colors. Father sent him there hoping it would improve his behavior and his attitude—but it just made him more resentful."

"I probably wouldn't be able to tell...." She examined the photograph carefully.

"I know," Daniel said, cutting her off.

"What's with the photo?" she asked, handing it back to Daniel. "Did you show it to your father?"

"No," said Daniel. "I wanted to, but, Amy, he just wasn't open to the idea. And what's worse..." Daniel sighed and shook his head.

"What's worse?" she asked, her tiny mouth opening into a perfect "o,"

"As I said, he's worse," replied Daniel. "God, Amy, he seemed better. He was talking up a storm, arguing, being his old obstreperous self. Then I talked with his physician and he says Father is worse. He says he has only a few months—maybe only a few weeks." Daniel stared at her and let his words sink in.

"No," she said, her brow wrinkled in concern. "I just don't understand how he can he seem better if he's really getting worse."

"The doctor says...hell....Vickers says it's because he's rallying for me. For my benefit. He would do that." He continued to slowly shake his head.

"So...so...what are you going to do? How does this affect your plans regarding David?" she asked in a careful, slow voice.

"I think it makes it even more important that I proceed with my plan—and right away." He lifted his coffee cup to his mouth and peeked at her over the rim.

"And us?"

"I can't tell him now. I told you about his plans for me and the neighborhood society belle, didn't I?"

"Yes, and I don't like it at all." She pushed her nose in the air and stuck out her chin, arms crossed.

"Oh, Sweet," he said, cajoling and grabbing her hand, which she removed from his grasp. "I have absolutely no interest in any other woman...." He let go of her when a man appeared at their table.

"Amy, I hope you're not bothering Mr. Bridgewater," said the large bearded man, wearing all white—trousers, shoes, shirt, apron, and puffed chef's cap. "Maybe, he'd like a piece of pie with his coffee."

"Sam," said Daniel, greeting the cook and diner owner. "Amy's actually keeping me company. She's helping to get me motivated to get back to the plant and work on the payroll."

"Payroll!" spouted the large chef, "Ach! Worst part of owning a business!"

"Don't I know it!" answered Daniel, laughing with Sam.

"I'll bring you some pie, Mr. Bridgewater," said Sam, "We have some nice peach and cherry. Would you like ice cream? On the house, Mr. Bridgewater. It's an honor to have you eating here."

"Best food in the county, Sam," said Daniel, beaming at the chef, "and best service too!" he added, smiling at Amy. "But actually, coffee is just fine. I'm not very hungry today."

"Amy, you work on him," said her employer, "Nobody can resist our pie. You know it."

"I will, Sam," answered Amy, smiling at the chef, who was heading back to the kitchen.

"And don't pester Mr. Bridgewater, Amy," he yelled at her as he departed, "Let him eat in peace."

Amy and Daniel laughed and smiled as they watched Sam exit. Then they turned back to each other and returned to their earlier conversation.

"You were saying about…other women?" asked Amy, eyebrow raised.

"I was saying there are no other women for me," he whispered and pulled her close to him across the table.

"Okay, okay," replied Amy, a reddish color flushing across her cheeks, "don't get all mushy on me here at work." She patted his cheeks with her hands and he pouted out his lips in a routine that had obviously occurred before. "So, what's your next step, Mr. Bridgewater?" she asked grabbing her order book from her pocket along with her short pencil.

"My next step is to find David," he replied, placing the small photo in the middle of the table and placing his index finger on it like an arrow. "Wherever he is."

"You really think that will please your Father?"

"I don't know if it will please him, but I have to do it and I have to find him before Father dies."

"And, if what you tell me is true, that could be sooner rather than later," she whispered gently.

"Yes. Listen, I know this means delaying dealing with our situation—with Father. I hate leaving you in limbo like this. Oh, God, I wish Father weren't so difficult. In so many ways, he's a wonderful man. Truly. You'd love him, I think if you got to know him and he got to know you in a gradual, normal way. But to thrust this situation on him when he's ill and when the situation with David is up in the air—I'm afraid it would push him over the edge. I'm afraid it would kill him."

"Believe me, Dan, I understand. I don't want to be responsible for anything happening to your Father. I'm patient. After all, I waited—how long?—for you."

"You did, didn't you? And I'm worth it, aren't I? It will work out, Sweet. Just let me find David first."

"How are you going to find him? Where do you start?"

"Vickers is going to help me. He's got an investigator."

"Like a private investigator?" she asked, eyes widening in excitement.

"Right. Just like a crime show. Surely, his trail can't be that cold. Surely, if someone who knows what they're doing starts looking, they can track David down."

"Where do you think he could be?"

"Who knows? Maybe overseas. Maybe in New York. I mean he was always interested in the arts. I guess he might go to an arts center."

"Maybe," Amy said. She looked at Daniel. Her mind and heart were full of conflicting emotions. She was excited about the prospect of hunting down David. She was a very curious person and was always up for a challenge. She wanted to know where David was for Daniel's sake more than for his father's. Daniel seemed to really need to know his whereabouts. But she was worried too. She was worried about Daniel's father. Of course he was old and old people died, but Daniel felt responsibility for his father and if he did anything—or revealed anything—to his father that upset him and precipitated his death, Daniel would probably never forgive himself. She couldn't have that happen. Some things could be kept secret from Daniel's father. But finding David and revealing his location to Daniel's father—or even bringing him to Daniel's father—that was a dangerous step. After all, David left under very unpleasant circumstances and had made no attempts to contact Daniel or Charles over the years. Trying to find him might not be the positive move that Daniel assumed it would be. It might backfire in ways that Daniel might not be able to anticipate at the moment. Unfortunately, there wasn't much she could do about any of it, except support Daniel—and she would. And wait—and she would. But not forever.

Chapter 7

Present time--Sunday evening, December 16

"Local disc jockey murdered on air. Our top story on Channel Three News Tonight—your earliest and best news of everything happening in Reardon."

"Rocky!" yelled Pamela into the kitchen as she stood in the couple's living room staring at the photograph that filled the television screen. "Rocky! Come here! They're talking about that disc jockey!"

Rocky's head popped out the kitchen door. He held a large wooden spoon in one hand and a dish towel in the other.

The television screen cut to a close-up of a young anchor woman.

"Local disc jockey Theodore Ballard of radio station KRDN was shot and killed on air early this morning—shortly after midnight, according to local authorities."

Rocky moved into the living room, closer to his wife as they both stared at the screen, which now showed an outside shot of the small radio station, standing alone in a field of grass, its call letters on a sign almost larger than the station itself.

"Ballard was working alone at the KRDN studio on Highway 27, south of Reardon, when an unknown assailant entered the studio and shot him in the head," continued the anchor in voice-over mode. The screen changed to a poor quality shot of Ballard, obviously cropped from a group picture. "Ballard's body was discovered this morning around 12:30 a.m. when station manager Roger Gallagher and local police entered the unlocked studio."

"That photograph is probably pretty old," said Rocky, "he doesn't look very Goth there."

"No," said Pamela, "no eye liner or weird hair." In truth, Pamela was amazed with how totally ordinary Theodore Ballard looked. A bland, sort of round face. No particularly striking features. Certainly, he wasn't ugly—just not very memorable.

The anchor then cut to a field reporter standing outside the radio station who reported on police efforts to solve the baffling crime, then conducted a quick interview with the aforesaid station manager Roger Gallagher.

"Mr. Gallagher, you found Ballard's body?"

"Yes, I was asleep. The police called me shortly after midnight and asked me to meet them at the station. When I got here, the studio was unlocked. When we went inside, we found Ted lying on the floor beside the mike."

"Mr. Gallagher, do you have any idea who might have done this?

"None, but it's very scary. I always thought, we always thought our dj's were perfectly safe working here alone—at night. We're obviously going to have to rethink our policy now." The camera panned to Gallagher's distraught face.

The story ended with a plea to viewers to call the Reardon police if they had any information that might lead to the apprehension of the killer or killers of Theodore Ballard.

When the story was over, Rocky flipped off the TV and headed back to the kitchen, followed by his wife. As he worked preparing their Sunday evening meal, she assisted by setting the table.

"So," she said to him, "after everything we've learned today from Trudi, and from that TV report, do you have any thoughts?"

"What about?" he said, turning to her as he continued to stir a mixture on the stove. "You mean, am I trying to ferret out the killer? I leave that to you, my dear."

"I'm thinking," she mused, as she distributed silverware around their dining room table, "of the likelihood of this being some random killing? You know, someone just going crazy and stopping by the radio station and shooting the first person they see. When Charlotte was killed last year, everyone thought that was what happened at first. They couldn't imagine anyone intentionally killing her. Now this killing, to me seems even less like a random shooting. What do you think?"

"I don't know," he answered, "I'm not really thinking about it—other than it's awful." He reached in the cupboard and brought out several bottles of spices.

"It seems quite premeditated to me," she said, stopping at the table and staring out the dining room window. The leaves outside were swirling and the wind was whipping up. This was about as much winter as they got this far south. She often wished they would just once in a while get a little bit of snow. It would make December seem truly Christmas-y.

"How so?"

"If a madman goes crazy, he's more likely to go someplace where there's lots of people. This killer went to an out of the way radio station where only one person was working late on a Saturday night. For all he knew, nobody would be there."

"Not true," answered her husband, reaching into the oven and peeking at his peach cobbler that had been bubbling and sending out a heavenly aroma now for at least an hour. "If the killer followed the station's programming schedule, he would know exactly what time people would be there."

"Which would mean premeditation, right?" she asked, continuing to place plates and glasses at the three spots around the table.

"I suppose," responded Rocky, now plating items in serving bowls. "Can you get Angie? I've about got this all ready."

"I'm here," announced their sleepy daughter, stretching her arms and yawning as she sauntered down the hallway, followed by Candide.

"Homework?" asked her mother, placing salt and pepper shakers in the center of the table.

"Done. One two-page essay for English. Twenty-four boring problems for Math, and a fill-in-the blank conversation about railroad stations for French: 'Est-ce que le train pour Rouen départ a dix heures?' Doesn't that all sound exciting?" asked Angie, wearing jeans and a neatly pressed t-shirt and her newest pair of sneakers. Her hair was combed and clean.

"Your timing is perfect," said Rocky, bringing the serving dishes to the dining room. "Dinner is served. Have a seat." He placed the dishes on the table. There was a glistening pork roast with a raisin sauce, broccoli almondine, mashed potatoes with garlic, and, of course, the cobbler for dessert. Yes, thought Pamela, she could not skip the gym tomorrow.

"You're rather dressed up for a Sunday dinner at home," said Pamela to her daughter.

"I'm going out later," responded Angela, piling food on her plate. It annoyed Pamela (although she would never say it) how her thin daughter could eat anything and never gain an ounce of fat. Candide sat expectantly by Angela's chair, primed for any falling morsels.

"Where are you going?" asked Rocky. "It's a school night."

"Just to the library," answered Angela. "Kent's picking me up in a little bit."

"The purple-haired kid?" prodded her father, an annoyed sharpness to his voice. "The one who takes you to murder scenes?"

"Dad!" said Angela, sneering. "I thought we went over all of this."

"We did, Angie," said Pamela, placing her hand on Rocky's arm and giving him a stern look. "Remember, dear, Kent is my graduate assistant. He's very responsible and conscientious. We agreed to that I thought."

"All right. All right," Rocky answered, sighing and tearing into his pork with gusto.

"Did they find the guy who killed Black Vulture?" asked his daughter.

"Who?" asked Rocky, almost choking on his food.

"Black Vulture," repeated Angela, "Ted Ballard, the disc jockey. Did they find the person who killed him?"

"Black Vulture? That's his name?"

"His Goth name," replied Angela.

"Not yet," said Pamela, "but it's been on the news. Hopefully, anyone with any information will come forward."

"I hope so," said Angela, nibbling on the broccoli without much enthusiasm. "He was a good dj. I really liked his program. It was the only radio show that played any good alternative music."

"Really?" asked Pamela. "There weren't any other stations that played this—what do you call the type of music he played?"

"Some people call it Goth," answered Angela, "some, alternative rock. There are lots of names and really lots of different styles. But Black Vulture—I mean Theodore—knew them all. He really investigated the different bands and introduced a lot of new groups on air. Kent liked him too."

"Why did they call him Black Vulture?" asked Rocky.

"I don't know," said Angela. "A lot of people in alternative music have alternative names." She was moving the broccoli around on her plate, possibly in hopes that it would disappear by itself.

"Did you ever see this Black Vulture, Angie?" asked Pamela, eyeing her daughter's food machinations.

"No, Mom, I've just heard him on the radio," answered her daughter, "but Kent's seen him. He's seen him at the Blue Poppy."

"The Blue what?" asked Rocky, taking his empty plate and his wife's empty plate to the kitchen. He remained there as he started to scoop portions of peach cobbler into bowls.

"It's a Goth club in downtown Reardon," said Angela. "You know, a few blocks down from the Factory." The Reardon Coffee Factory, known to locals as "The Factory" was the most famous eatery in the area. Its standard fare of sandwiches and salads wasn't what brought in the crowds. No, the Factory sat on the site of one of the few original coffee substitute plants in the country—this one founded by Romulus Reardon to brew potable beverages from various plants for the Confederate troops during the Civil War.

Customers came from around the globe to sample the various coffee-like drinks.

The doorbell rang and Angie leaped up from her broccoli manipulations, while at the same time dropping a small piece of pork down to Candide, and ran to answer it.

"Hi!" she said, greeting a young man standing on the porch, dressed in similar garb--jeans, sneakers, and a t-shirt. His spiky hair had twinges of purple throughout.

"Hey," responded Kent Drummond to Angela.

Pamela walked to the door behind her daughter and greeted the young man.

"Hi, Kent," she said, "Won't you come in?"

"Hey, Dr. B," replied the young man, "Angie and I are just going down to the library for a few hours, if that's okay. I've got that paper of yours I need to work on and she has a research project she needs to get started on too. If that's okay with you?"

"Yes, of course it is, Kent," said Pamela, as she led the young couple back to the dining room. "Why don't you have a seat first and join us for dessert? My husband just made some peach cobbler."

"Great, sounds good. Hey, Mr. B!" he yelled his greeting to Angela's father who he could see in the kitchen.

"Hello, Kent," answered Rocky, bringing in several bowls of cobbler topped with scoops of vanilla ice cream. "Here you go." He placed the desserts in front of the two young people and handed Kent a spoon. The two college students immediately began gobbling down the dessert. Rocky returned to the kitchen and came back with cobbler for his wife and himself. For a few moments all was quiet as all four ate in silent pleasure.

"So, Kent," said Pamela, almost finished with her cobbler, "I understand from Angie that the two of you heard the murder of this Ted Ballard last night. She says you even know him."

"Dr. B, "began Kent, "I hardly know him. I maybe saw him once or twice at the Blue Poppy downtown. I did listen to his program on Saturday nights, but I never spoke to him or anything like that. I guess you could say I was a fan. It really sucks what happened to him."

"Yeah," agreed Rocky, "being shot in the head would suck quite a bit I would think."

"Do you think he had any enemies?" asked Pamela.

"I wouldn't know," responded Kent, attempting to squeeze in bites of cobbler while he answered the questions of his major professor and the parents of the girl he was dating. "I can't imagine anyone. It's pretty awful."

"Yes," agreed Pamela. "Awful."

"Okay, Mom," interrupted Angela, "are you through grilling Kent? We need to get to the library." She eyed the young man, quizzically.

"Right, oh, right," he said, nodding at Angela. "That was absolutely delicious, Mr. B. Fantastic! We'd better get going now, though. Okay, Angie?"

"Okay, let's go," Angela responded, and the two of them gathered their winter jackets and headed out into the wind and cold.

After they left, Pamela remained seated at the table. Rocky brought them both coffee and they sipped the warm liquid in companionable silence.

"Just how serious is this relationship, do you think?" asked Rocky. "Is that what you're contemplating so intently?" He grabbed her hand and gave it a quick kiss.

"Oh, no," she said. "I wasn't thinking about Angie and Kent. They're a nice young couple. Actually, Angie is lucky to have someone like Kent take an interest in her. He's extremely responsible."

"Yeah, yeah," he replied with great vocal exaggeration, "the most responsible graduate assistant you've ever had! But I'm not sure that sterling assistant translates into safe boyfriend for my nineteen year old daughter."

"Rocky," she said, smiling at him, "I love how protective you are of Angie, but truly, she has never given us any reason to worry. She may be sullen and morose, but she's always been responsible."

"So far," he said.

"And that's all we can go on," she responded, kissing his cheek. "Actually, what I was thinking of was who could have killed this Ted Ballard."

"Oh, no!" he moaned. "Not again! Please don't get involved in another murder investigation, Babe! You almost got yourself killed last year, sticking your nose into Charlotte's murder."

"For heaven's sake, Rocky," she chided, patting his cheek. "I'm not going to do anything dangerous. You know how careful I always am. But, what would it hurt if I poked around just a little? What could it possibly hurt?"

"Famous last words," said Rocky.

Chapter 8

The previous week--Wednesday morning, December 12

Harold Vickers bumped into Daniel Bridgewater as Harold was entering the Bridgewater Carpet Company office. Daniel was just leaving at high speed and putting on his winter jacket as he went.

"Harold," he said, spying the company lawyer, "walk with me, will you? I'm on my way to the plant. There's some sort of equipment problem."

Vickers turned and walked beside Daniel, increasing the size of his steps to meet those of the younger man. The two men stepped out into the cold December air and immediately rounded the fountain which guarded the entrance to the main building. They followed the main entrance driveway to a turn-off road on the left leading to the plant.

"Daniel, I only just stopped by to tell you I've found you an investigator."

"Good," answered Daniel, not slowing his pace. "Did you tell him to call me or should I make an appointment with him?" The wind nipped his cheeks and Daniel dug his hands deeper into the pockets of his jacket.

"Actually, I met with several candidates and this fellow seemed the most qualified," added Harold, puffing in the cold air and his attempts to keep up Daniel's pace. "I've got his business card for you. You can contact him and set up an appointment when you're ready."

"Good," said Daniel, as the two men reached the entrance to the plant, not more than 100 yards from the main office, but strategically placed behind several rows of trees to hide its less attractive front from the more impressive appearance of the main office building. "Come in with me, will you?"

"Sure," responded Harold, as the two men entered the side entrance door of the large windowless warehouse-like structure. The pneumatic door swung closed slowly behind them as they enjoyed the warmth from inside and removed their outer garments. Inside the noise of the carpet-making machinery made talk almost impossible.

"Mr. Bridgewater," called out a man dressed in a blue work shirt and jeans, heading towards them. He shook hands with Daniel.

"Jim," Daniel said, "What's up?"

"Howdy, Mr. Vickers," said Fredericks, greeting the lawyer, "but, hey, Mr. Bridgewater, it's really just a mechanical malfunction---nothing legal, really."

Daniel laughed and placed his hand on Frederick's back. "Harold's just with me on—other company business, Jim. Tagging along." All three men laughed.

"Let me show you the problem, Mr. Bridgewater," said Fredericks after a moment, and motioned for the two men to follow him. They walked quickly down a center aisle of mechanized carpet-weaving equipment, churning out waves of industrial and residential carpet by the miles. The machines rose to the ceiling of the giant warehouse and the movement of the newly-woven carpet flowing out the ends of each machine looked like colorful ocean waves hitting the shore. The sound resembled the ocean too—only much louder.

Eventually the three men stopped at a side aisle where Fredericks turned and strode between a row of smaller machines. These were not ceiling height but were still monstrous and noisy. When they reached the end of the aisle, near the outside wall, one large machine painted green sat idle—a large swatch of beige carpet bent over on itself within its long, central opening. It looked like a big green dragon with prey stuck between its teeth. The three men looked up at the strange sight.

"That's stuck, all right," said Daniel.

"Yeah," said Fredericks, "The engineers have tried rerouting the computerized signal. Tony's been up there with a knife trying to clear the grip. Really, we've tried about everything we can think of, Mr. Bridgewater. I'm about ready to call the manufacturer, but you know from past experience that they're usually not much help." He shouted this to the two men because the noise from the machines that were still working was deafening.

"I know," said Daniel, peering up at the carpet segment stuck in the gears. "It would be days before they could get someone here and even then, there's no guarantee that they'd be able to fix it."

"We haven't given up, sir," said Fredericks, "but I thought you should know."

"I'm glad you called, Jim," replied Daniel, still staring intently. "You said Tony was up there already?"

"Right. He poked around. It's probably some sort of jam, but he couldn't dislodge it." Fredericks pulled out a rag from his pocket and wiped his forehead. Although nippy outside, it was warm in the plant. Harold listened to the two men discuss the nature of the piece of broken equipment. Although this was certainly not his area of expertise, he knew that broken equipment could cause major delays and thus major loss of income in the carpet manufacturing business. Most manufacturers had onsite staff to handle repairs for just that reason. So far, Bridgewater Carpets had been lucky and had never suffered a major equipment failure. One reason for that was that Charles Bridgewater, and now obviously his son, Daniel, always took a personal, hands-on interest in the running of the factory.

"Give me that vice wrench and the pliers," said Daniel to Fredericks. Vickers wasn't certain he'd heard the young CEO correctly, but Fredericks handed the tools to his boss. Daniel slipped the wrench into his belt and held the pliers in his left hand.

"You sure the power is off?" Daniel asked Fredericks, as he grabbed the side of the large loom.

"Yes, sir," said Fredericks, "but, sir, you shouldn't risk...." But it was too late. Daniel had leaped up on the machine and was climbing it in monkey fashion to the top of the loom where the obvious pile up was preventing the carpet from progressing through the loom. When he reached the site of the problem, he examined the stuck carpet, lifting the portion he could, high so he could peer underneath. He stuck his head underneath the problem section of machine and over it, obviously examining the jam from every angle possible. Finally, he removed the wrench from his pocket and attached it to a side metal bar next to the carpet jam. Then, using the pliers, he pulled a small section of the carpet from the underside, up and over the top segment. Then, he twisted the wrench and rolled the side metal pipe in the opposite direction. While holding the metal pipe with the wrench in his left hand, he used his right hand to pull the underside carpet piece out from the top piece. With a snap, the underside piece ripped loose and the tangled carpet piece suddenly lay straight. Then, he tightened the side metal bar back to its original position using the wrench and replaced the tools in his belt. Scooting quickly down the piping backwards, he turned to Fredericks and said, "Okay, power her up. Let's see what happens."

Fredericks removed a walkie-talkie from his belt-clip and pressed a button, "Hey, Mike, power up Number 41." Immediately a light on the large machine gleamed green and the large mechanized roller slowly began to turn. The stuck piece of carpet popped once, then smoothly began to flow from the loom and out over the stretcher bar where it then began rolling onto a large cardboard tube for storage.

"Success!" said Daniel.

"Mr. Bridgewater," said Fredericks, "you saved us a lot of time. Thanks!" He shook Daniel's hand.

"No problem, just glad it worked," he said to his foreman. Then, he turned to Vickers. "Let's head back to the office. I want to call this PI." The two men headed out of the factory and across the company grounds.

"You obviously missed your calling," said Vickers, in admiration.

"Father made me learn every aspect of the business—including the workings of the plant. I spent many summers atop those machines."

"You might have been a sailor up on the riggings," said Vickers, as they again passed the fountain and headed into the main office building. "I probably should see that you get some sort of hazardous duty insurance if you're going to be climbing all over large industrial equipment."

Daniel laughed. "If you do, don't tell father. He thinks fixing equipment is all just part of the carpet business."

"I didn't realize until today what a dangerous business it is," said Vickers.

"Harold," said Daniel, "the carpet business is one of the most benign, least threatening, least glamorous businesses there is. That's probably one reason David…oh, never mind." He waved his hands briefly in front of his face. The two men entered the lobby of Daniel's office on the second floor. Vickers was winded from the trip back but Daniel was energized.

"Bernice," said Daniel to his secretary, "would you bring us some coffee, please?" He removed his coat and laid it on the secretary's desk.

"Yes, sir," replied the middle-aged secretary as she quickly rose and went to prepare a tray of coffee cups, a pot of coffee, a creamer, sugar, and spoons. The two men entered Daniel's private office. Daniel settled into his desk chair and Vickers removed his jacket and placed it over an arm chair in front of the desk. He then sat in the chair with an exhausted sigh.

Bernice entered with the coffee tray which she placed on the desk. Daniel served Vickers, knowing from experience that he preferred it black with two sugars. The men sipped and enjoyed the warmth of the office and the brew for a few moments.

"So," said Daniel, finally, breaking the silence, "let's see that business card."

Vickers reached into his pocket and removed his wallet from which he withdrew a small rectangular card. He handed it to Daniel.

"Sylvester Jax," said Daniel, reading the imprint. "Private Investigator. And you think he's the best?"

"Of the ones I interviewed," replied Vickers.

"Missing persons, fraud, identity theft," read Daniel. "Well, he seems experienced in a number of areas. Let's give him a try." He picked up the receiver of his office telephone and dialed the number on the card. After a few rings, there was an answer.

"Mr. Jax?" asked Daniel. When he was assured that he was addressing the private investigator himself, he continued speaking, "My name is Daniel Bridgewater. I'm President of Bridgewater Carpet Manufacturing. Our company lawyer Harold Vickers has recommended you for an investigating job. I understand he spoke with you recently. Yes. I was wondering if you might be able to come to our plant? No, it's not a business investigation. Actually, it's quite personal, but I'd rather discuss it with you here in my office than at my home. I believe you'll understand when I explain the particulars to you. You could? That would be excellent. See you then."

"He's going to do it?"

"We'll see. I hope. If he doesn't, I will."

"Daniel..."

"Harold, I'm going to find David—one way or the other."

Chapter 9

The present--Monday morning, December 17

It had been such a hectic weekend that Pamela was finding Monday actually restful as she relaxed on her office sofa, munching a crunchy Mexican veggie roll-up that Rocky had made for her. She always enjoyed peeking in her brown paper bag to discover what treat her husband had concocted for her to eat each day. He also provided her with a thermos of herb tea; today's specialty was pomegranate and he'd slipped in a chocolate coconut bar for dessert. She was in heaven—her mind far, far from the sordid doings that had consumed her interests yesterday.

Then she thought about the poor disc jockey. Another death in just over a year. No, this hadn't really occurred on campus, but the victim was a student—and an instructor. It brought back to Pamela in vivid detail the days last year when she had discovered the body of her colleague Charlotte Clark strangled to death with a cord from a headset in their computer lab.

Her students this morning were all agog with tales of the disc jockey who had been murdered while on air. She didn't mention to them her own personal involvement in the case—what with Rocky having to go down to console Trudi Muldoon and then, on top of everything, to run into Detective Shoop. What were the chances that he would be working this case! He had given her nothing but trouble during the investigation of Charlotte's murder. Of course, she mused, he was there at the end. Which was a good thing, she thought, otherwise the killer would have made her his second victim. Luckily Shoop and his men had arrived in time and saved her. She probably shouldn't be so hard on him, but she just couldn't help it. He stood in her way at every turn, trying to prevent her attempts to...to...to...what? she wondered. To solve the mystery, she realized. He probably just wanted all the glory for himself. Oh, that's ridiculous, she realized. He was just doing his job—and part of his job was to protect me. After all, I am a civilian. Shoop wasn't used to a civilian trying to solve a crime. He kept ordering her to cease and desist. She laughed to herself. I guess I was a bit headstrong, she thought. Oh, well, there's not much I can do with this case. Rocky may know the victim—or at least he knows somebody who knew the victim—as she remembered Trudi in her office, but I don't know the victim at all.

Just forget the whole thing, she told herself. Let life get back to normal. She probably wouldn't hear any more about it except on the news. Just as well. She had more than enough to do with her job. She had classes to teach, papers to grade, research projects to complete, and articles to publish.

"The last thing I need is another murder," she said out loud as she rolled up her paper lunch bag and scored two points as she landed it squarely in the middle of her waste basket on the other side of her desk.

"Another murder?" called out a friendly voice, as a woman's head peeped around the door frame. Her neat white bob and stylish glasses framed a lively face, sparkling with good humor. "Don't tell me you're investigating again?" asked the woman as she rounded the door and entered the room. She remained standing in the doorway, one hand pressed against the frame.

"Joan," replied Pamela, as she raised her arm and motioned the woman into her office. "You heard me thinking out loud."

Joan Bentley strode into her office a few steps and stood with her hands on her hips.

"I certainly hope you're not thinking of getting involved in this disc jockey murder," said the older woman, her eyes glaring at Pamela, her brows raised, suspiciously.

"Of course not," said Pamela, "that's the furthest thing from my mind." She leaned back on her blue and pink paisley couch and sipped from her thermos.

"Bravo," said Joan, with a curt nod, as she sat primly on the straight back chair by the door. Joan Bentley's outfits always seemed to match her demeanor—today's was a colorful suit, a subtle mixture of greens and yellows, with a trim white blouse and respectable low-heeled shoes. She placed her grade book and her pen on her lap.

"Although…"

"Although what?" asked Joan, leaning towards Pamela, her arms suddenly crossed firmly.

"Although Rocky knew the victim."

"You don't say."

"I do. He was a doctoral student in English—one of Trudi Muldoon's advisees. Rocky's office is across the hall from Trudi's."

"So Rocky had spoken with this fellow who was shot?"

"Oh, no, nothing like that. He just recognized the name when they reported it on the news. Then, yesterday, Trudi called and we went over to Silverton and sat with her while the police went through this Ballard guy's office. She had to wait because the police wanted to question her more."

"My goodness, my dear," said Joan sitting up straighter, "you just seem to run into crime wherever you go." She made that "tsk-tsk" sound with her tongue.

"You're not kidding," said Pamela, bending closer to her friend and whispering, "guess who's the lead investigator on this case?"

"Not your old friend?"

"Yup," said Pamela, nodding, "Detective Shoop. Maybe he's Reardon's only homicide detective for all I know." She laughed and Joan joined in. As they were giggling together, another woman stomped into the room.

"What's so funny?" asked the tall, lanky young woman, her thick, curly, black hair flopping in her eyes as she looked from Joan to Pamela. "I obviously missed a great joke."

"Pamela's embroiled in another murder mystery," said Joan, in a secretive whisper to the newcomer.

"Joan," chided Pamela, "I am no such thing. Hi, Arliss. I assume you've heard about the disc jockey who was killed at KRDN?"

"I heard. How does that concern you, Pam?" she asked as she rounded Pamela's desk, pulled out the rolling chair, and plopped herself down and her feet up on the desk.

"It doesn't," responded Pamela, sipping her tea. "Rocky knew him. He was a doctoral candidate in English."

"No kidding?" asked Arliss, leaning back as the rolling chair moved back and forth from the desk. "Hmm. Not good." She crossed her arms and appeared to ponder the news.

"Arliss?" questioned Joan.

"What?"

"You're very quiet," answered Joan. This was an understatement, thought Pamela, as Arliss MacGregor was usually the most outspoken and opinionated friend she had. Joan and Pamela spent a good portion of their time trying to calm Arliss down when she was in one of her frenzies—usually about the state of the Psychology Department's animal lab, of which Arliss was director.

"Trying to make a decision," responded the young instructor, swaying back and forth on the desk chair, her feet planted firmly on the desk top. Pamela always was careful to clear her desk top of important papers before she moved to the couch to eat lunch because she knew Arliss liked to relax in this position and Pamela did not want Arliss' feet to damage any of her research. Of course, Pamela could have lunched at her own desk, but she far preferred sitting on her couch, which she did most of the time—unless she was working on her computer.

"All right," said Pamela, setting down her thermos on her end table by her sofa, "what decision?"

"What to do about Bob," answered Arliss. Bob Goodman was the department's animal psychology director and Arliss's immediate supervisor. They worked together closely. Just how closely, Pamela discovered last year during her "investigation" of Charlotte Clark's murder when she overhead Bob and Arliss in a romantic tete-a-tete under the central stairwell. The couple had been involved for quite some time but had kept their relationship secret until that point. Pamela had "outed" them. Ever since, Joan and Pamela had teased Arliss mercilessly about Bob, but Arliss remained discreet. The fact that today she was even mentioning the name of her paramour was a shock to both women.

"What about Bob?" asked Joan. Both Joan and Pamela leaned towards Arliss, in eager anticipation.

"He---he—asked me—he asked me," said Arliss, flinging her feet back on the floor, and attempting to swallow.

The other women waited for her to complete her sentence.

"He asked me to....," said Arliss, kicking her loafers back and forth on the linoleum under the desk and scrunching her brow.

"For God's sake," said Joan, finally, "What?"

"To marry him," squeaked Arliss, deflated, staring at her shoes.

"To marry him?" asked Pamela, "My God, Arliss, you sound as if he asked you to dig ditches with him."

"He asked you to marry him?" repeated Joan. "Like—get married, have a wedding, go on a honeymoon, marry him?" With each phrase from Joan's mouth Arliss' face fell noticeably and her shoulders drooped.

"Is there any other kind?" she asked, with a look of complete dejection.

"Okay," said Pamela, nodding slowly, "I hear you, but I'm not understanding. I'm sensing that you think marrying Bob is not a good idea. Is that it?"

"I don't know," said Arliss, still sitting with her body crumpled, staring at the ground.

"Now, wait a minute," said Joan. "You never discuss this—your relationship with Bob—with us. You always say you don't want to talk about it. Does this mean, you want our advice, or what?"

"I don't know," repeated Arliss.

"Joan," said Pamela, turning to her friend, "whether she wants our advice or not, I think we need to help her. I mean, look at her. Have you ever seen her like this?"

"No," said Joan, "she looks like one of her rats—a scared little rat."

"My rats are not scared!" piped up Arliss, now in fight mode as the subject turned to one on which she felt more at home.

"So," said Pamela, stretching out her left index finger and pressing it with her right index finger, "let me get this straight. Bob proposed to you and you said 'I don't know'?"

"Sort of," responded Arliss, swishing her feet back and forth under the desk.

"For heaven's sake," said Joan, "stop dancing around over there, and concentrate." Arliss looked at Joan with a start and quickly brought her feet together, her entire body straightening. "Now, how long have you and Bob been—dating?"

"I don't know," Arliss started to reply, then added, "several years."

"Several years?" asked Pamela, "surely you know by now if you want to marry him or not. Do you love him?"

"Of course, I love him," said Arliss. "but, why should that matter? Lots of people who love each other don't get married."

"True," said Joan, nodding wisely, "but, I suspect Bob isn't one of those. He always strikes me as very traditional."

"He is," said Arliss, pouting.

"So," continued Joan, "you would prefer to live in sin indefinitely?"

"Joan!" gasped Pamela, shocked at her older friend's lack of delicacy with their younger colleague.

"Is that so horrible?" Arliss peeked up and looked back and forth between her two friends.

"It's certainly fine with me," answered Joan. Joan was probably the more "liberated" of the three of them, Pamela realized. She did not let being a widow stand in the way of her enjoyment of life.

"It's fine with me too," said Pamela, "but we're not the ones who matter, Arliss. Bob is the one who matters. He obviously wants to get married or else he wouldn't have asked you."

"I know," said Arliss, "he's so...so..... He gave me this." She scrounged around in the pocket of her loose trousers and brought out her fist, which she held out in front of the two women and then opened abruptly.

"My God! It's the Hope Diamond," exclaimed Joan, as she admired the beautiful and very large stone on the delicate gold band. "You're carrying it around in your pocket?"

"I don't feel comfortable wearing jewelry," said Arliss. A watch is all I really need.

"Believe me, Arliss," said Pamela, "no one needs a diamond ring. But many of us enjoy getting them, just the same. I have one. Joan has one. Does that make either of us any less of a liberated woman in your eyes?"

"No, of course not," said Arliss, "I'm not opposed to rings or weddings or marriage in principle—just not for me."

"All right," said Joan, "we can discuss this; we can, dear. But first, please, put that rock away somewhere safer than your pocket or put it on your finger."

"Okay," said Arliss, reluctantly, placing the ring on her finger, "just until I decide what to do with it." She put the ring on her right thumb and folded her other fingers over it.

"Arliss," said Pamela, "let me ask you this. Do you anticipate this living in sin relationship with Bob to continue indefinitely?"

"I'd be happy if it did," she replied.

"Do you think that's fair to Bob?" asked Pamela. "He obviously loves you and wants the two of you to be together permanently. If you reject him..."

"I'm not rejecting him," whined Arliss.

"Maybe not," added Joan, "but I'm sure it feels that way to him."

"What horrible catastrophe would occur if you married Bob?" asked Pamela.

"I don't know," said Arliss. "But what good could come from it?"

"Where are you living?" asked Pamela, glaring at Arliss.

"You know where I live, Pam," said Arliss, scowling, "you've been to my apartment enough times."

"You don't live with Bob?" asked Joan, aghast.

"No," responded Arliss, "I have an apartment. You know that."

"And in your apartment you are not allowed to have pets," said Pamela, ignoring Joan, "if I recall correctly."

"So?" replied Arliss defiantly.

"Just a thought," said Pamela, casually, "but if you and Bob were married, if you lived together, you might consider purchasing a house—maybe even a farmhouse—there are some nice ones on the outskirts of Reardon—where pets are not only allowed, they are encouraged—lots of pets."

"I'm thinking," said Arliss, biting her lip and pushing her unruly hair out of her eyes again.

"Just a possibility," said Pamela.

"Right, my dear," chimed in Joan, "don't throw the baby out with the bath water. Haven't you always wanted some larger animals—not just a dog and some cats? I know you've discussed horses."

"Stop," said Arliss. "This is cruel. I need to think."

"Thinking," said Detective Shoop, appearing suddenly in the doorway, obviously having overheard the three women talking.

"My, my!" exclaimed Pamela, "Detective Shoop! What brings you all the way over to my office. I thought you and your men would still be digging through clues at Silverton Hall or at the radio station."

"My dear, Dr. Barnes," he said politely to the professor on the couch, as he gave her a sweeping bow, "we have completed our collection of evidence at the station, at Ballard's office, and at his apartment, and are now hard at work going over the clues. I stopped by your office because I have a favor to ask."

"Do tell, Detective," said Pamela, smiling, "and what favor could I possibly do for you?" She crossed her legs, swinging her top leg back and forth coyly.

"Actually, Dr. Barnes," continued the tall, gangly man, his overcoat swinging as he spoke, "it occurred to me yesterday when I saw you in Dr. Muldoon's office that the two murders—that of this Ted Ballard and that of Charlotte Clark last year have certain similarities."

"Really, Detective?" said Pamela, blinking quizzically, "what similarities would those be?" She ceased the swinging leg and planted her feet on the ground.

"Both murders were recorded," responded Shoop. "Charlotte Clark's murder, of course, was recorded accidentally and was only retrievable by your department, but Ted Ballard's murder was heard by a live audience and was recorded automatically by the radio station where it occurred."

"That is an astounding observation, Detective," answered Pamela. Joan and Arliss were listening and watching the charged interchange between their friend and the austere looking policeman. The more Pamela sparkled, the more distressed it seemed the detective appeared.

"I just happen to have a copy of the recording of Ballard's murder that was made at KRDN," said Shoop as he removed a CD box from his inside pocket. "Possibly, you might enjoy analyzing it as you did the recording made of Charlotte Clark's murder."

"Detective Shoop," said Pamela, beaming, "are you asking me to help with your investigation?"

"My dear, Dr. Barnes," replied Shoop, giving her a curt bow, "I'm no fool. I will take all the help I can get—and as it appears unlikely that Ballard's killer will be coming forth and confessing in the near future, if you are able to supply us with any clues regarding his identity from the sounds on this tape, I would be forever in your debt."

"My goodness, Detective," said Pamela, "of course, I will be happy to listen to the recording. I can't promise anything, but I will give it my best try."

"That's all I ask, Dr. Barnes," said the man, handing her the CD. "That's all I ask."

Chapter 10

Previous week--Wednesday, late, December 12

Amy Shuster turned off her little portable television set on which she had been watching the local news in her small living room and shuffled into her even smaller bedroom to get ready for bed. She set her alarm clock for six a.m., knowing she was working the early shift the next day at the diner. Giving her cat Tinkerbelle a quick shove off of her quilt, she pulled down the coverlet, removed her toasty robe and slippers, and scooted under the sheets. Tinkerbelle howled in annoyance but marched off with her typical haughty attitude to her own bed in Amy's small kitchen.

"Not tonight, Tink," said Amy to the departing feline. "I'm way too tired for your shenanigans." It was true. She was exhausted. The diner had been packed, but she was glad to have kept busy because Daniel had not been there today. She'd heard some of the plant workers who were eating there talking about a broken piece of machinery that was slowing down production. She figured that was what was keeping him busy—that and his dying father and trying to track down David. Oh, well, she thought, I can't see him every day. Even so, she missed him, badly.

She turned out the lamp on her nightstand and the little room was plunged into darkness, except for the light from some of the downtown businesses. Amy's apartment was above a hardware store in Compton and some stores kept their signs lit—even at night. She had tried nightshades, curtains, Venetians blinds—but nothing kept out all the ambient light. Just adjust. Her mother had always said that's what people did. If you couldn't solve a problem—maybe it wasn't that bad of a problem and you could learn to live with it. All in all, a little outside light coming through her window at night wasn't really the worst of problems—and she had learned to adjust. She was very much like her mother—very practical. She wished her mother were alive now. She had a lot she wanted to discuss with the wise woman. Just how practical was she being? Amy wondered.

Along with the outdoor lights came the noises—cars, a stray dog, people yelling at each other every so often—downtown sounds. Amy had learned to tune them out—just like the light. She had learned to focus on what mattered—and when she focused on something—there wasn't much that could distract her. It was hard to clear her mind for sleep; she kept contemplating the concerns that faced her—Daniel, his father, Daniel's determination to find David, their relationship. Daniel intended to solve each problem in a particular order—David first, then his father, and finally their relationship. Amy understood his reasoning but she wasn't certain she agreed with his reasons.

Tinkerbelle jumped back on her bed. It was hopeless. "Tink, are you lonely too?" The big calico purred and snuggled against her body, then—bored—leaped down and headed out into the front room. Amy reached for the long gold chain around her neck and followed it down to the small bauble at the end. She sighed as she touched the delicate keepsake in the dark, running her finger around the small circle she now had grown to know so well. She was so used to how it felt but not very used to what it looked like as she touched it more often than she looked at it. It was almost as if, bringing it out to look at it was bad luck—so she kept it tucked away on the chain where she could feel it always with her.

A noise in the living room drew her attention. Was that Tinkerbelle? Possibly the old yellow tabby was sneaking around her apartment looking for some hidden treat and had knocked over a knick-knack. It had happened before. No, wait. That sounded more like the front door opening. But, she had locked the door before she went to bed, she was sure. She clutched the covers around her shoulders and sunk down further as if to hide from any potential intruder. The door clicked again and footsteps tip-toed towards the bedroom. Her bedroom door cracked open and a figure moved towards the bed and leaned over her.

"I missed you today," said Daniel, his cheek nuzzling hers.

"Dan," she shrieked, sitting up, "you scared me! You're ice cold!"

"I'm sorry, Sweet," he embraced her, sitting beside her on the bed, "I tried to get away, but there was a malfunction at the plant and then another set-back with father and—oh—just a terrible day."

"Your father?" she asked, her arms on his, "how is he?"

"Holding his own," responded Daniel, "but obviously, not doing well. Makes me even more determined to track down David." He removed his gloves.

"Have you made any progress?" she asked.

"Let me tell you," he said, as he took off his jacket and placed it over an arm chair in the corner of the bedroom. He sat down next to her. "I have an appointment with an investigator tomorrow, so things are starting to move."

"That's good," replied Amy, shivering next to the cold from Daniel's body. "Here, let me warm you up." She wrapped her arms around him and they remained entwined and silent for a few moments. As his eyes adjusted to the darkness, Daniel reached for Amy's face and placed it in his hands.

"You're so beautiful," he whispered, gazing at her. "Like an angel in the moonlight."

"More like a frazzled waitress in the light from the sign from McNally's Hardware," she laughed. He kissed her gently and then more passionately.

"Wait," he said as he quickly slipped out of his clothes and slid under the covers beside her. "Better." They hugged tightly until both were warmed by the bed and the body heat.

"So," she said, "What's this I heard about you climbing up some sky-high loom?"

"My god," he moaned, "don't tell me that's traveling around now?"

"My heart was in my stomach when I heard it."

"Some carpeting just got stuck in one of the rollers. I climbed up and extracted it."

"With your teeth?" she said, purring and poking his ribs.

"I save my teeth for nibbling," he responded and began rubbing his lips over her belly.

"No, really," she insisted, "what did you do? I had no idea you could repair those big monster machines. I thought you sat behind a desk all day."

"Didn't know I was so macho, did you?"

"No," she said, teasing, "I thought you were Casper Milquetoast."

"Who?"

"Casper..." She swatted him playfully.

"Never mind. Never mind. I know who he is. And I am not one. I am a hero, at least—your hero."

"Always," she squeezed him tightly. "And you don't need to climb tall buildings or machines. You don't need to do anything except be you."

"That I can do," he said, caressing her hair.

"And your father?" she questioned. "You said there was a setback?"

"He had some sort of seizure," said Daniel, "They gave him a shot of something and it calmed him down. Even so, afterwards, he was still talking to me. Not as much as yesterday, but he was still there, Amy. He's trying so hard to hang on. Maybe he knows I'm trying to find David."

"Even though he says he doesn't want you to look for him?"

"It's his pride. It's all his pride," he sighed. "David's departure obviously hurt him deeply. If I can find David and bring him back—just think what that would do for father."

"If you can find him," she cautioned, "If you can bring him back."

"That's why I'm hiring this Jax," said Daniel in Amy's ear. "Tomorrow."

"Tomorrow," she replied, "and maybe the tomorrow after that we can tell your father about us if he withstands finding out about your search for David?"

"It is the absolute next item on the agenda. Reunite father with David—then drop the bomb about us."

"I hope he survives all these surprises and revelations." She put her head on Daniel's chest.

"He's tough. He's shown me that at every turn. I just have to hope he will hang on and that he'll realize that all of this is good news—and he'll be happy about it."

"Dan," she said, worried, "what's good news for you isn't necessarily good news for someone else."

"I refuse to believe that," he said, defiantly.

"Ever the optimist," she said, shaking her head, "and it worries me. Either way, it's getting late and I have to be at work at six. I need to get to sleep."

"You do?" he asked.

"Yes." She pulled on her chain and felt the circle at the end. She grasped it tightly in her palm, as if for good luck.

"This instant?"

"Soon," she said. His nose rubbed her bare shoulder as his leg encircled her torso. She reacted by wrapping her legs around his waist and tightening her arms around his neck. "But not immediately," she said, as the chain fell between her breasts.

Chapter 11

Present time--Monday afternoon, December 17

As soon as Shoop and Joan and Arliss had departed, Pamela wasted no time in loading the compact disc into her hard drive and bringing up her acoustic analysis program. She set her volume at a moderate level in case any people in the hallways might be listening. Even if they were, strange sounds often emanated from Pamela's office as she frequently listened to peculiar sounds—human and non-human alike—for her academic research. Last year when she was analyzing the sounds that had been recorded during the murder of her colleague Charlotte Clark, she went to great lengths to disguise her efforts. Now, she didn't even think twice about listening to the recording of the murder of the disc jockey. If truth be told, she was probably not the only person with such a recording, she reasoned. Anyone who'd been listening to KRDN Saturday night with recording capabilities on their iPod or radio might very well have a similar recording.

She brought up the spectrograph on her monitor and set her cursor to the far left. As she opened the recording, a peaked line, something like a read-out from a seismograph filled the screen. She pressed "play" and the voice of the disc jockey, Theodore Ballard, could be heard. As he spoke, the cursor—which took the form of a vertical line that completely segmented the spectrograph from top to bottom—moved rapidly from the left of the screen to the right—where it ended abruptly. Pamela reset the cursor and pressed "play" a second time.

The recording lasted around seven minutes and included songs introduced by Ballard as well as his patter between.

Some of the comments Ballard made, she realized, were enlightening as far as providing information about Ballard's background. However, it was unlikely that the entire seven minutes of the recording would produce much evidence regarding the killer. No, she thought. I'd better focus—at least for now--on the segment where the killer enters and the actual murder takes place. By repeating the tape again, she located the exact spot where she believed the killer must have actually come in the door of the studio. A few seconds before the killer's entrance, she realized that Ballard was aware that he had a visitor but had no idea who the person was. Ballard gave no indication of knowing the person on the tape. That is, he didn't call the person by name or show by the way he spoke that he had any relationship with the killer at all. This is going to be hard, she thought.

All right, she said to herself. Let's start with the obvious. Let's see if I can find out anything from the killer. I wonder, she mused, if the killer made any noise. On first (and second and third) glance it didn't appear so, but she reminded herself that Ballard was sitting behind the microphone and the killer was standing in the doorway. If the killer spoke at all, Ballard's microphone which was probably uni-directional would not pick up the sound very well. But, she reasoned, that doesn't mean that I can't hear it. She set the cursor at the segment where she believed the killer entered and punched in directions for her analysis program to run a low pass-filter. Then, with her eyes on the cursor, she pressed "play":

> "Oh, hi! Come on in! I'm Theodore Ballard—Black Vulture to my fans. You a fan of alternative rock? What the? That's a gun! What do you need a gun for? Why're you pointing it at me? Wha--? No! No!"

The blast of the gun shook her as the acoustic profile of the explosion filled the screen. "Okay," she said, "let's see if there's any sound hiding in the background. Using her cursor to zero in on various peaks and waves in the acoustic profile before her, she highlighted a segment below the regular line of Ballard's speech. This small, faint wave appeared immediately after Ballard had said, "alternative rock" and before he said "What the?". The acoustic program revealed that the segment lasted a fraction of a second. She set her cursor on the small wave and highlighted it. When she pressed "play" the overlapping sound of Ballard's speech was eliminated and the only sound audible through Pamela's desktop speakers was the brief sound of what seemed like a gasp. Yes, it seemed like a gasp, she thought. The strange sound must have come from the killer because it would have been impossible for Ballard to produce a totally separate sound wave while in the process of speaking something else. To verify this, she decided to establish an identity profile for Ballard and the suspect sound. This was a procedure that she had developed in the course of her research on vocal linguistics. All voices varied and those variations could be identified acoustically. Some variations occurred across individuals depending on various factors such as emotion, age, gender, geographical location, and a variety of other features. That is, there were certain acoustic features that all men shared—acoustically--and all women, just as there were certain acoustic features that tended to appear in all people as they got older. But there were other acoustic features that discriminated between groups. Some researchers were primarily interested in the similarities (or differences) of a certain group. Others—like Pamela—were interested in using acoustic technology to identify specific individuals. Her research and that of others like her had been instrumental in helping develop protocols for using acoustics to aid in criminal investigations as well as many other areas where the ability to identify a person was crucial. Her students had taken what she had taught them and had gone on to acquire interesting careers using this very technology.

 Now that she had separated the suspect sound—the one she believed belonged to the killer—she worked to amplify the sound and stretch it out so that she could investigate each part of it and ultimately try to identify the killer. Of course, she realized that it would probably be unlikely that she would be able to actually identify the killer because the concept of identification implied that there was a pool of suspects from which to choose. As far as she knew, no such pool existed. Even so, she believed she might be able to provide some clues for the police—something she might discover from this short gasp that the killer had probably uttered just as he (or she—a woman could wield a handgun just as well as a man) revealed the gun.

She pressed "play" again and the brief sound jumped from her speaker. Yes, it did sound like a gasp. She felt certain it wasn't a word. It didn't sound as if the killer was attempting to speak. Maybe it was a snarl or a growl. She kept imagining what the killer might feasibly say or mutter just at the moment of revealing the murder weapon. As she played the sound again, she had the sense that the killer was gasping. She could hear what sounded somewhat like an intake of air. As air passed through the vocal folds, no sound was actually produced by the larynx. There was something registering on the spectrograph so some laryngeal activity took place—something like the killer producing intake of air while producing an open vowel such as "o" or "ah." Unfortunately, no actual word appeared to be said. Even so, the small voiced vowel gave her something to go on as far as identifying the killer. It was extremely soft, far away, and very short, but she marked the wave and recreated it in an accompanying analysis program. Here she asked her software program to tell her what the fundamental frequency was. Soon she knew one thing about the killer, she was sure. It might be the only thing she would ever know from the acoustic output, but it was more than the police probably had. Pamela Barnes was quite certain that Theodore Ballard's unknown killer was male.

She was so totally engaged in her investigation of the murder tape that she didn't notice when Willard Swinton, one of her colleagues entered her office, puffing.

"Pamela!"

"Willard," she said, looking up at the older African American gentleman, leaning somewhat uncomfortably on his silver-topped cane. Always nattily dressed, Willard today sported a dark green suit with a bright yellow vest. His curly hair with a few wisps of grey topped his perfectly round head. "Come, look at this, will you?"

"What have you got?" asked Willard with excitement. The two researchers had often collaborated on various linguistics projects. Willard was an expert on accents and regional dialects. If anyone could recognize a particular voice and where it was from by just a brief gasp it was Willard. He rounded her desk and peered over her shoulder at the array on the screen.

"See this segment," she said, pointing out the brief wave she had just listened to.

"What is it?" he asked.

"Let me tell you that after you hear it," she said, coyly. She pressed "play" and the enhanced gasp was audible and then immediately disappeared.

"That's it?" asked Willard. She nodded. "Again," he directed as Pamela repeated the sound.

"Not much to go on, is there?" he asked her.

"No, but, anything you can tell me, Willard....."

"I'd say, from the quality of the vowel...definitely Southern...."

"And male, right?"

"Oh, yes, male."

"Southern meaning local? From around here?"

"I wouldn't say that. I don't think I can pin it down that much from just 'ah'"

"What kind of man is it?" she asked.

"You expect a lot from just a vowel, Pamela. What project is this for, anyway?"

Pamela looked at the door and then back at Willard standing beside her. She motioned him down and whispered in his ear. "It's a recording of the murder of that disc jockey at KRDN on Saturday night. You heard about it, didn't?"

"How could I not? That's all the students are talking about. But, I don't get it. Why just the one vowel? If this guy was a disc jockey don't they have a longer recording?"

"Not him, Willard. I think—I'm not positive—but I think this gasp—or vowel—might have been from the killer—not the victim. The police can't identify him and they asked me to listen to the recording and see if I could discover anything about the killer."

"My goodness, Pamela, you do get yourself into the middle of things, don't you?"

"I do, don't I?" she responded smiling.

Willard hobbled to Pamela's couch where he carefully lowered himself. "My dear, I can't say much more from just those few repetitions of that vowel, but if you'd be so kind as to make me a duplicate CD, I would be ever so delighted to join your efforts in crime detection and see what I can do to assist you."

"You would?"

"Of course," he replied, "That last caper of yours I only got to experience at the very end when the police stormed your office and saved you at the last minute from the dastardly villain." Pamela smiled brightly at him, opened her desk, removed a blank CD and quickly duplicated the original CD and handed it to Willard.

"Welcome aboard, detective," she said, handing him the CD, eyebrows raised.

"I will treasure this disc and guard it with my life," he said.

"You don't need to do that. Just see what you can figure out about that gasp—and anything else about the recording that you can."

"You have my word."

With that, he lifted his body with difficulty, leaning on his cane and headed jauntily down the hall, whistling.

Chapter 12

Previous week--Thursday, morning, December 13

"Good morning, Mr. Bridgewater," greeted Bernice, his secretary as Daniel strode towards his office, his face buried in a folder.

"Good morning, Bernice," he replied. The darkly-dressed woman started to rise hesitantly, clearing her throat.

"How is your father, sir?" she continued. Daniel stopped beside her desk and smiled.

"He's holding his own, Bernice," he said, "thank you for asking."

"Mr. Bridgewater," she said, clutching her wool skirt, "Everyone here is concerned about Mr. Bridgewater. He's in all our prayers."

"Thank you, Bernice," said Daniel, closing the folder and leaning over her desk, "My father considers all of you—all of the employees of the company his family. I know it means a lot to him to know you all care about his welfare."

"We do, sir. We do," she said, nodding. Daniel smiled again, hesitated and then abruptly continued towards his office. At the door, he turned and said, "Oh, Bernice, I'm expecting a Mr. Jax sometime this morning."

"Yes, sir," she replied crisply and returned to typing at her computer.

Daniel entered his office. At once, silence surrounded him. The small noises of the outer office—typing, printers, and the soft music wafting throughout the main office facility—were no longer audible. He sat at his desk and reached for the photograph album that had remained on the left-hand side since the previous day. He removed the photograph he had taken out yesterday from his inside suit coat pocket and open the album to the page from where it had come. Looking back and forth between photo and page, he contemplated the pictures—and people—represented. The intercom on the right hand side of his desk buzzed and he responded.

"Yes, Bernice?"

"Mr. Bridgewater, Mr. Jax to see you."

"Send him in."

"Yes, sir." Immediately the door opened and Bernice ushered in a short, middle-aged gentleman carrying a brief case. He looked for all the world, thought Daniel, more like a banker than a private investigator. A navy blue pin-stripe suit, a red tie, and a crisp white skirt with honest-to-god cufflinks constituted his outfit. Daniel hadn't seen any one wear real cuff links in ages.

"Mr. Jax?" questioned Daniel, his hand extended, walking to the man.

"Mr. Bridgewater, delighted to make your acquaintance, sir." Jax provided a perfunctory handshake and remained standing until Daniel escorted him to one of the chairs facing his desk.

"Have a seat."

"Thank you, sir," replied Jax, placing his briefcase on the floor beside the chair and sitting formally in the leather chair, knees together and feet on the floor and together. "Now, I understand from your attorney, Mr. Vickers, that you would like me to undertake a private investigation involving a family disappearance." Jax raised his arms and pulled neatly on the cuffs of his shirt.

"Yes, true," answered Daniel, "Just how much did Harold tell you?" He leaned back in his chair and twisted his pen back and forth.

"He gave me the basics, I believe," said Jax, smiling a little half-grin, "at least as far as he knew. Before I came, I did a preliminary check to see what was available in public records." He lifted his briefcase from the floor, opened it, and removed a thin folder.

"On David?" asked Daniel. Jax thumbed through several items in the folder.

"Yes," said Jax as he glanced at one of the documents in the folder, "Mr. Vickers, as I said, provided me with the pertinent background information, so I have the birth certificate, obviously…"

"Obviously…

"It appears we have extensive records for David up until about—let's see—" he paused as he flipped over one of the documents and ran his finger down a list of items, "1997. Does that seem right?"

"Probably," responded Daniel, his brain trying frantically to keep up with the little man's speed. "Yes, 1997 would be about the time he…disappeared."

"Disappeared?" asked Jax, setting down the folder on Daniel's desk and posing his pen as if to write, "is that actually what happened?"

"He did disappear," said Daniel.

Jax set down the pen and looked directly into Daniel's eyes. "There is disappear and there is *disappear*, Mr. Bridgewater. Mr. Vickers was not terribly clear as to any particular cause for David's…disappearance. I was hoping you might be more enlightening." He pulled his suit coat as if straightening it, gave a bit of a shrug, and faced Daniel with a smile, his eye lids partially closed—somewhat like a cobra.

"There is really no great secret, Mr. Jax," said Daniel, "There was quite a row between David and my father—Charles Bridgewater. They disagreed about many things—in particular David's chosen career path. David fancied himself an artist and my father fancied him a business man. This was right after my mother's death."

"Your mother died how?"

"In a car accident. She was driving; David was in the passenger seat. He was in the hospital with broken bones for several days afterward."

"So, soon after your mother's death, David abruptly leaves home and your father disowns him—or your father disowns him and he leaves home."

"I really can't say, Mr. Jax. It all happened so fast and nobody at the time kept me informed of what was going on.

I know what I know from what I overheard. My father refuses to talk about it."

"I can see how all this has been a source of great family friction," replied Jax, now running down a list in his folder with his gold fountain pen. "If I am to track down David, sir, it would be helpful if I could interview your father…"

"That's not possible," said Daniel, quickly. "My father is quite ill and is in no condition for visitors, Mr. Jax. I'm afraid you'll have to make do with me. I will certainly try to answer any questions you have."

"Yes, sir," said Jax, "but, truly, if I could question Mr. Bridgewater, if only for a minute or two—to discern the nature of the disagreement.…"

"Mr. Jax," repeated Daniel, now becoming noticeably frustrated, "as I said, that is impossible. The doctor only lets me visit him for a very brief time each day. This morning when I was there, Father hardly recognized me. I'm sure he would never let a stranger see him and upset him—which I guarantee your questions would—you'll just have to trust me and the information I provide you."

"Yes, sir," said Jax, with a sigh of resignation as he picked up the folder and returned to what was obviously a list inside. "I merely thought that if he wanted me to track down David that he would wish to speak to me directly to…"

"Mr. Jax," said Daniel, leaning over the desk and whispering, "My father did not initiate this investigation—I did. He has no idea I am even conducting it. Truth be told, if he did know—he would probably not approve. He might even.…" Daniel stopped himself before he finished the sentence, turned and looked out his bay window.

"Mr. Bridgewater," said Jax, after a moment, as Daniel gazed silently out at the fountain in front of the building, "are you really certain that you want to pursue this investigation then? With your father so sick.…"

"Mr. Jax," replied Daniel, turning back to the man sitting in front of his desk, "I am even more determined to find David. My father may not have hired you or even wanted to hire you, but I believe in my heart that finding David is the best thing I can do for him. I have no way of convincing you of my sincerity…"

"It's not your sincerity of which I need convincing, sir," said Jax, in a calm but authoritative voice, "it's your wisdom."

"You're not the first person to tell me that," said Daniel, chuckling. "All right, all right, I'm a fool, but I'm going to find David and if you won't help me I'll just find another investigator.

"Oh, I'll help you, sir," replied Jax. "I just wanted to be certain where you stood. I can see where that is. I don't want to waste my time for a client who isn't motivated."

"Thank you, Mr. Jax," said Daniel, "I guarantee I am motivated. I've got to find David—and I've got to find him soon."

"Yes," replied Jax, staring intently into Daniel's eyes. Then, suddenly, he opened the folder, ran his finger down his list and spoke officially, "So, let's see, a few more questions. I understand from Mr. Vickers that you can supply a photograph…"

"Yes," replied Daniel as he opened the album and removed the photograph that he had been carrying with him for the last day. "This is David at his high school graduation in 1997."

"Hmm, yes, I see," replied Jax as he glanced back up at Daniel. "Have you received any correspondence from David since then? Any letters? E-mails? Packages? Anything?"

"No," replied Daniel, shaking his head, his shoulders dropping, "nothing in twelve years. He just seemed to have vanished."

"He might be—I'm sorry to suggest this—but, he might be dead," said Jax.

"I realize that," answered Daniel, "and if he is, I want to know that. It's not what I'm hoping for, but at least it would be closure."

"I understand, sir," said Jax, "and I certainly hope that I will be able to provide you with a more agreeable outcome." He replaced the folder into his briefcase and closed it. "I believe I have all the information I need to get started, sir. If

I need any additional information, I assume you will not object to my contacting you directly?"

"Of course not," said Daniel, rising as Jax rose, "Here's my card, the bottom number reaches my office directly and let me give you my cell phone number," he said as he quickly jotted an additional set of numbers at the bottom of the card and handed the card to Jax.

"Thank you, sir," he said and turned to leave.

"Let me walk you out, Mr. Jax," said Daniel as he escorted the little man to the door. The two men exited the building and around the fountain.

"Lovely fountain," said Jax as they passed the massive structure, "totally unexpected, I might add."

"Yes," agreed Daniel, laughing, "Some people consider it an eyesore, but I have mixed feelings. My father built it in honor of my mother. It was modeled on a fountain she had fallen in love with in Italy on my parents' honeymoon. David always loved it too. It was probably the only thing he did love about Bridgewater Carpets."

Chapter 13

Present time—Monday, late afternoon, December 17

Willard had been gone for a while, and Pamela was still at her desk, listening to the disc of the murder at KRDN. She had not gotten any further. Indeed, she was now uncertain about her earlier conviction that the faint vowel sound overlapping Ted Ballard's speech that she thought was spoken by the murderer really was. At least she was uncertain about the gender conclusion she had drawn; the more she listened, the more she thought the short sound might be female. If this were the case, Willard's deduction about the speaker being from the south could also be suspect, although it was probably more likely that whoever the killer was, he or she was southern—just by a process of elimination. They did, after all, live in the South, and most people here were Southerners. Would a Northerner travel all the way down here to murder a local disc jockey?

So many questions. She was getting no where. She glanced at her watch and realized it was after five o'clock. She had become so engrossed in her analysis that she had completely blocked out the sounds of the students going in and out of the lecture hall next door. Now, she realized that it must be around five and students were starting to exit into the hallway.

She continued replaying the recording. The more she listened, the more she realized her difficulties. With the recording she had made last year that captured the murder of Charlotte Clark in the departmental computer lab, there was no speech—only weird sounds—scrapes, bumps, choking, clicks, and other strange noises--that ultimately turned out to be Charlotte's efforts to keep from being strangled to death by the murderer—also a member of the department. Pamela's analysis of the sounds on the recording had finally led her to one sound that the killer had made with a remote control device while strangling Charlotte and had ultimately resulted in his arrest. At the time last year, Pamela was actually annoyed that Charlotte had not said anything on the recording—not that a person can say much when they're being strangled. But Pamela's specialty was the acoustic analysis of voices—and she did this best when she had actual speech with which to work. She had none for Charlotte's recording—and still had managed to identify the killer. Now, here she was with speech on the suspect recording, but unfortunately, it was speech of the victim—with the possible exception of that short gasp or grunt—just a vowel that might prove to be produced by the actual killer. It was more information than she had had with Charlotte. Would it be enough to identify the killer?

The students were now mostly gone from the lecture hall. She heard the footsteps coming down the hall of someone she knew well. Rising and going to the door, she called:

"Mitchell."

"Pamela," said Mitchell Marks, Chair of the Psychology Department at Grace University and Pamela's immediate superior. Mitchell had taken over teaching introductory psychology lectures last year in addition to his duties as chair. Evidently, Mitchell enjoyed working with the mostly freshman students, as he had again scheduled himself for the two back-to-back classes on Monday. "You're here late," he said to Pamela as he passed her office door.

"Waiting for you," she replied. "Can I walk with you to your office?"

"Absolutely," said Marks, a fairly tall man, with wavy blond hair and grey-blue eyes. Pamela ejected the CD from her computer, shut down her hard drive, grabbed her purse, keys, and jacket and, after locking her door, followed Marks down the hallway.

"I've got to thank you, Pamela," he said, as he held open the corner stairwell door for her. The twosome entered the stairwell. Their voices echoed against the concrete walls. "I never knew how much I would enjoy teaching that intro class. And that was your suggestion."

"You're welcome," she replied, "I can hear them from my office, you know. So I know how they're responding to you."

"It's really just the perfect respite after a long day of administrative duties," he sighed. "There's just never an end to all the squabbling between administration and the rest of us, is there?"

"Luckily, Mitchell," she said, smiling at him as his long strides swept them out onto the first floor and down the main hallway towards his office, "we have you to deal with administration for us."

"Smart," he responded, nodding, holding open the door to the main office of the Psychology Department. Pamela entered and followed Marks into his office which was through a small alcove where the departmental secretary maintained her desk.

"Jane Marie," he announced to the pert brunette sitting at her computer, "I'm going to be talking to Pamela for a while. Please don't let anyone disturb us." He escorted Pamela in. Pamela turned back just in time to see Jane Marie give her a curious look and a shrug. Then Marks closed the door behind them and immediately strode to his large desk.

Pamela selected one of the four chairs in front of Mitchell's desk. Mitchell's office always intimidated her. It was one of the largest offices in the building—probably on campus—not necessarily because Mitchell was any more important than any other department head, but Blake Hall, home of the Psychology Department was one of the oldest buildings on campus, and many of the offices and classrooms had been reconfigured from an earlier time. Pamela guessed that Mitchell's office had once been some sort of dining room or library in an old mansion. The ceilings were higher than other offices and certainly higher than any of the classrooms. Bookshelves rose to the ceiling—so high that Mitchell needed a traveling ladder to reach the top shelves. There was one long dining-room sized table on one side of the room and two desks on the other—

the one at which Mitchell sat to greet faculty and students—and the other that held his computer and printer and related paraphernalia. All around the room—in the shelves, on window sills, and hanging from walls—were memorabilia. Many of these were academic—plaques, certificates, and awards from Mitchell's many years of scholarship and research. However, there were also many natural trophies—stuffed animal heads, ducks, geese, and guns—everywhere. Mitchell was an antique gun aficionado and she had heard many tales of his hunting exploits at faculty meetings and dinners.

"So?" he asked, leaning back in his rolling, reclining leather arm chair. "What can I do for you?"

"Guns," she said.

"Guns?" he asked. "Don't tell me, Pamela, that you're taking up hunting?"

"Not quite," she responded. "But I need to pick your brain about weaponry."

"Interesting," he said, nodding. He grabbed a pencil between his palms and rolled it about, peering at her as he rocked back and forth.

"Mitchell, I'm afraid, I've gotten myself involved in another mystery," she said, finally.

"Oh?" Mitchell rubbed his hand through his thick blond hair.

"Yes, and—I might add—not by my own choosing."

"Your husband will be glad to hear that."

"He doesn't know—yet."

"Hmm. And I'm to assume that you're not going to tell him?"

"No, I'll tell him--eventually," she said. "Detective Shoop came by my office today and asked for my help in their investigation of the murder of that local disc jockey that happened Saturday night. Did you hear about it?"

"Oh," he said, stopping his chair from rocking and planting his feet on the ground. He leaned his elbows on his desk and bent forward towards her. "I believe I did. My students were talking about it today."

"Yes," she said, "they would. Anyway, the poor guy was shot while he was on air Saturday night—on KRDN. Shoop is the lead investigator. The station records all their programs so they obviously had the recording of the murder itself. Shoop brought me a copy of it to see if I might do an acoustic analysis—like I did with Charlotte's murder—and maybe help them identify the killer."

"So, they don't know who the killer is," said Mitchell.

"Not a clue," she said, "I mean, KRDN is just a small, little isolated building out there on Highway 27. This Ballard—the disc jockey—was the only one there Saturday night—when the killer walked in, shot him dead, and left. No one evidently saw the person or has any idea who it is."

"You said guns?" prompted Mitchell.

"Yes," she replied, setting her jacket and other belongings on a nearby chair, and bringing the CD in its sleeve out from her purse. "I've been listening to this all during my office hours today. Willard is helping me too, but our expertise focuses on voices. There's obviously Ballard's voice and we think we might hear the killer's voice superimposed over some of what Ballard says. I'm still working on that. What I wanted to ask you about is the gunshot. That's something I know nothing about. Nothing at all. I thought you might play the CD and just give me your impressions."

"Sure," said Mitchell, reaching for the CD, "let's crank 'er up." She handed him the CD. He removed it from its sleeve and inserted it into his hard drive. Then, he pressed "play." The now familiar sound of Ted Ballard's voice filled his office:

> "Oh, hi! Come on in! I'm Theodore Ballard—Black Vulture to my fans. You a fan of alternative rock? What the? That's a gun! What do you need a gun for? Why are you pointing it at me? Wha--? No! No!"

At that point, the gunshot exploded from Mitchell's monitor and then the sound stopped.

"That's it?" he asked.

"That's it," she answered.

Mitchell replayed the final moments of the recording several times so he could hear the gunshot.

"Obviously," he said, finally, "it's a hand gun—not a rifle. But beyond that, there's not much I can say just from listening to the sound. To tell the truth, Pamela, if you asked me to identify this gun by looking at corresponding bullets or bullet holes in animal carcasses—or almost anything like that, I'd be able to do the job for you."

"No, don't apologize, Mitchell," she said, "if you're sure it's a handgun and not a rifle, believe me, that's more than I can determine from it. And, of course, Shoop will probably be able to pin it down more when he gets the autopsy results. I was just curious. It helps me try to picture what was happening. Now, I can envision the killer, maybe with a handgun in his pocket—which makes sense. It would be much harder to disguise or hide a rifle."

"I wish I could tell you more about the gun," said Mitchell, "but I can't just with a few times through. Maybe if I could continue to listen to it and think about it…"

"I don't see any reason why…"

"A copy?" he asked.

"I gave Willard a copy so he could help me. If you want a copy, I don't see a problem. After all, any one listening to KRDN Saturday with a recorder running might have a copy of the murder too."

"Here," said Mitchell, opening a lower left-hand drawer in his large desk, "I'll make it myself." He re-inserted the CD along with a blank disc from his desk and clicked "duplicate." Soon, the computer spit out both discs. Mitchell replaced the original CD in its sleeve and returned it to Pamela. "I'll listen to it again. Maybe I can find something. After all, why should you be the only member of the Psychology Department to solve all the crimes?" He smiled warmly and she smirked.

"It's no great honor," she said.

"Gives me something to do now that there's no longer anything exciting happening in our department."

"There is the wedding," she said, then immediately regretted her cavalier dispersion of Arliss's private issues.

"Wedding?" he asked, "What wedding?"

"Oh, god, I shouldn't have said anything," she moaned, head bowed.

"Cat's out of the bag now, Pamela," he scowled, arms folded, "Who in—let me think---in our department?"

She nodded, lips squeezed together.

"Willard and Joan? Hmm, no, unlikely. Phin is married. Laura is married. You're married. I know it's not me because I'm married. Must be—by process of elimination—Bob and Arliss." He announced the names and looked at her triumphantly.

"You knew already," she said. "I just found out today."

"A good department head knows everything about the members of his faculty," he said, slyly, blue eyes twinkling.

"Please don't tell Arliss I said anything." She stood and grabbed her purse and jacket to leave.

"Fear not," he answered, escorting her to the door, "I'm the soul of discretion."

Pamela beamed at him as he opened the door and stood there as she exited. Then he closed the door and she found herself alone in the secretary's alcove.

"Dr. Barnes," whispered Jane Marie, stopping her flying fingers from her keyboard. "That was some secret meeting."

"Indeed," she said to the friendly secretary, "Mitchell is always a surprise."

"He is, isn't he?" agreed Jane Marie, a candy cane posed between her teeth.

"Jane Marie," said Pamela, "did you hear about the disc jockey that was shot?"

"Of course, Dr. Barnes," she replied, "it was awful! Some of the students even heard it themselves. They were listening to the radio when he was shot!"

"My daughter was one of them," admitted Pamela to her friend.

"The poor girl," said Jane Marie, "It must have been almost like seeing it happen, don't you think?"

"Not quite," said Pamela, "Not quite."

"Have a candy cane, Dr. Barnes," said Jane Marie, holding up a mug of little red and white sticks. Grabbing a Christmas candy, Pamela waved farewell to Jane Marie and headed out of the main office and down the hallway to the side entrance to the parking lot.

As she walked towards her car, she tightened her jacket around her and put her hands in her pockets. A cold December day in Reardon. She glanced around and felt the leaves whip against her legs as she reached her car door. As she unlocked her door and crawled into the driver's seat, her cell phone rang. Now what? She thought.

"Yes," she answered. Only a few people had her cell phone number, and she didn't recognize the number on the caller ID.

"Dr. Barnes?" the voice asked.

"Yes," she answered. She knew the caller.

"Detective Shoop here, Dr. Barnes," he said. How did he get her cell phone number? "Dr. Barnes, you've had that CD of the murder for at least three hours now. Have you identified the killer yet?"

Chapter 14

Previous week--Friday, December 14

Daniel had just finished speaking with Fredericks at the plant. He was relieved to hear that all the looms were functioning properly and he wouldn't have to return and perform another single-handed rescue at the factory today. He had far more important fish to fry, he thought. Luckily, most of the time, the plant ran itself and he handled executive business and management decisions from the main office. Even doing his own work and his father's too, he still had time to slip out in the afternoon (and many evenings) to see Amy. And, he thought with warm delight, seeing her was what made each day special. Oh, he enjoyed managing the business and he certainly liked providing employment for his workers—he liked being perceived of as a benevolent boss. But Amy made him glow—she made him feel like what he was doing had a purpose. And now that his father was in such grave condition, his attention was focused on trying to track down David.

He had always hoped that David would return on his own and that his father and David would reconcile naturally. He just assumed that David would get tired of maintaining this distance and that he would eventually want to return home and that things would be as they were before—if he would just wait. Now, he realized that he couldn't wait. His father might die at any moment and David hadn't come back. For all he knew, David didn't even know that Father was ill. How could he? He might be anywhere—overseas—in the jungle, or a desert. Who knew? Who knew if David was keeping in touch with sources that would inform him of Father's condition? No, he couldn't take the chance. He would have to find David himself and bring him home. He owed it to Father. Father needed to see David before he died and David needed to see Father. They both needed to reconcile. Daniel had to make it happen—it was his top priority.

As Daniel was pondering his options, his intercom buzzed and Bernice informed him that Sylvester Jax was in the outer office and wished to see him.

"Send him in, Bernice," said Daniel. The office door immediately opened and the small, erect man entered quickly and headed directly to Daniel's desk where he deposited his briefcase and opened it, displaying a pile of documents.

"Mr. Jax," said Daniel to Jax, "don't tell me you've located David?"

"I have, Mr. Bridgewater," replied Jax, his proud smile and snake-like lids gleaming. "If I may..." He removed several documents from the briefcase. Daniel seated himself at his desk and prepared for what appeared to be—a show.

"It was difficult to pin him down at first," Jax began, "but once we found what he had done, it was easy as blueberry pie." A tasty metaphor, thought Daniel. It reminded him of Amy and he wondered what she was doing at this moment.

"How so?" he asked. Jax remained standing and held up each item from his case as if he were conducting a college lecture, complete with grandiose gestures.

"First," he said, his left hand sweeping over the document in his right hand, "we had to find out where he went when he left here in 1997. We contacted Dexter Academy to determine if they had ever received any requests for transcripts for him—and they hadn't—none."

"And that would mean?"

"To me, if a student's high school never gets requests for transcripts, it can mean one of several things—the student doesn't intend to go to college, the student doesn't intend to get a job where the employer would require transcripts, the student has died—unlikely I believed—or, the student has changed identities."

"And?"

"It was my assumption, Mr. Bridgewater, for a variety of reasons," said Jax, his smile beaming with pride, "that David changed identities. Possibly not right after Dexter Academy. It's possible that he worked at some menial jobs for a while—I'd be inclined to think he did, until he got on his feet and had acquired some money—but then, seeing as how he never contacted Dexter, I began to believe that if he proceeded at all with higher education, he must have done it under an assumed name." Daniel leaned back, listening to this tale almost as if he were at the movies.

"And you think he went on for a college degree?"

"Definitely," replied Jax, "from everything you told me about David, I felt certain that ultimately he would return to school. Changing one's identity isn't difficult at all—many people do it every day. The problem arises in avoiding any connection to the previous identity. If David wanted to continue his education at most four year institutions, he would need to produce a high school diploma. He could not do so in his new identity."

"So what do you suppose he did?" asked Daniel, now thoroughly engrossed in the little investigator's hypothesis.

"Once he established his new identity," said Jax, continuing his scholarly lecture by pacing in front of Daniel's desk, "it would not be difficult to take a course or two at a small community college—even without a high school diploma, particularly if he had an employment record. From there, he probably built up a transcript at one—or more—local community or junior colleges and then ultimately transferred those credits to a four-year college where he could have completed his degree in his new name."

"That's a lot of trouble to go through just to keep from being connected to us," said Daniel, his brow furrowing and a note of sorrow in his voice.

"Mr. Bridgewater," said Jax, placing the documents on the desk and sitting down in a leather chair in front of Daniel, "connected to you—or being contacted by you, I don't know, but he did not want to be found. I'm not sure how he will react when—if—you contact him." He paused and allowed Daniel a moment to process his words.

"Please, please, Mr. Jax," said Daniel, eventually, "Please continue, where is David?"

"Actually, he's not that far away," said Jax, "we were able to use some remarkable new facial recognition software to connect him to a photograph of a graduate student at a nearby university. We have a database of student photographs from university yearbooks from all over the United States. Obviously, if David were not enrolled in school, this procedure would not have worked, but I suspected, given what you told me about the conflict between David and your father, that we might find him still studying officially somewhere—and we did."

"So, he's in school?" asked Daniel.

"Yes," said Jax, handing him several documents, "graduate school. As we've traced his school records back—back under his assumed name you understand—he's switched majors a number of times—music, art, literature, but always in the humanities or fine arts."

"Yes," said Daniel, "that would be David, the sensitive artist. Never was interested in business, much to Father's dismay. They came to blows because of it many times."

"They would not be the first," said Jax, shaking his head sympathetically. "Let me show you," he said, pulling out a map, opening it, and spreading it out on the top of Daniel's desk. "Here you see Compton, where you are," he said, pointing to the small town where Bridgewater Carpets was located. "And here," he said, raising his finger slightly off the map and moving it a few inches to the west, "is where David is."

"So close?" asked Daniel, "I can't believe he's been there all this time."

"Not all this time," said Jax. "He's changed institutions a number of times—possibly to throw you off track if you'd been looking for him, but he's been here for a number of years. We've been able to trace him back through yearbook photos—not those individual ones—he never sat for those—but we did find him in a number of group shots where each person was identified. Also, we found some photos of him from the town's local press. Here they are. Take a look. Seems he's a minor local celebrity."

"Really?" asked Daniel, looking at the grainy photographs. "What type of celebrity is he?"

"He's a disc jockey. Goes by the name of Black Vulture—but that's his radio name, of course. His actual name—or rather his new name—the one he assumed when he dropped David—is Ted Ballard."

Chapter 15

Present time—Monday, late afternoon, December 17

"Detective," said Pamela into her cell phone, not quite believing that the policeman was actually contacting her so soon after handing over the CD for analysis. "I really haven't had much time to listen to the recording."

"But, you have listened?" he asked.

"Yes, a few times," she responded, shivering, as she continued to put her key in her ignition and prepared to leave the Blake Hall parking lot. "I'm going to need more information, however, before I can do a truly thorough acoustic analysis." She turned on her heater and jacked the thermostat up as high as it would go.

"What do you need?" he asked.

"I'd need to talk to someone who knew Ballard, if possible," she replied. "Also, I'd really need to actually see the studio—probably take some measurements, if possible."

"We could do that," he said slowly, snuffling, "in fact, why not now?"

"Now?" The heater was starting to warm her car's interior and her shivering began to subside.

"I'll contact the station manager and have him meet us there. I'll bring a measuring tape—I assume you don't carry one around with you?"

"No," she hesitated, "but I was just on my way home."

"If it's out of your way, Dr. Barnes...."

"Actually," she sighed, thinking aloud, "it's not all that far. At least it's in the direction I'm headed," she concluded. "How long do you think this would take?"

"You're the one who needs to see the studio—you tell me."

"All right. I'll meet you there. It shouldn't take too long," she agreed, "I'll call my husband and tell him I'll be a bit late."

"I'm sure he's used to that," said Shoop, a humorless chuckle in his voice. "You know how to get to KRDN? On Highway 27?"

"Yes, I've been by there—it's a little building—next to that big transmitting tower, right? Out in the boonies."

"I'm on my way," said Shoop as he hung up.

She took her transmission out of "park" and headed out of the lot. The campus showed all the signs of winter—never really what she would call December. The wind was swirling leaves on the street and the campus grounds. Students walking on the sidewalks were bundled in warm jackets and scarves—a few with gloves, heads bent against the force of the wind. Virtually no one this far south owned a real winter coat, although today they could probably use one. As Pamela wound around the narrow, tree-lined campus streets, she contemplated just what she might find at the KRDN station. At the moment, there really wasn't any need for measurements, but she knew that if she could see the station where the murder had actually taken place she would be able to get a better sense of what had happened and possibly be better able to make sense of any clues that might be lurking on the CD. The measurements were really overkill. She needed to know about the microphone Ballard was using and how far he was seated from it. She needed to know where the door to the studio was located and how far it was from Ballard. That is—she needed to know how far the killer was from Ballard when he entered the studio. If the small brief segment of sound that she believed to be the killer's voice actually was, then knowing exactly where it was in relation to Ballard would be helpful in determining other identifying features about the killer.

As she exited the campus grounds and turned onto Jackson Drive, the main thoroughfare of Reardon, she also began to realize that meeting Shoop at the radio station would be an opportunity for her to grill him about evidence the police had uncovered—if any. If Shoop expected her to provide him with clues to the killer—he'd better provide her with whatever he had found so far. She continued to drive—easily because it was only around four o'clock, and Reardon traffic wouldn't pick up dramatically for another hour or so. She could probably avoid calling Rocky. If the meeting at the station was short, she'd be home with plenty of time to spare and she wouldn't even need to mention her latest activities to her spouse. Lord knows, she thought, the minute he found out that she was again embroiled in another murder investigation, he'd hit the ceiling. They had fought continually about her involvement with Charlotte's murder. No, she concluded. I'd just better not mention it to him. At least not yet. The less he knows the better.

As she passed the outskirts of town, she turned right onto Highway 27, a few blocks before the turn-off to her own home. A mile or two down this country highway was where radio station KRDN had its small building. She saw the transmitter in the distance as she rounded a bend in the road. It was starting to get dark early now and the transmitter lights high up on the tower were twinkling red—on and off. Obviously KRDN had not let the murder of one of its employees stand in the way of its broadcasting schedule. She pulled into the small gravel lot in front of the little brick building. The KRDN sign on top was almost bigger than the building itself. Several cars were parked in front. She guessed that the old grey sedan belonged to Shoop. She locked her car and entered the glass door in front. Immediately she was in the studio proper. The studio was wood-paneled with large plate glass windows fronting on the parking lot. Below the windows were a row of straight back chairs. Pamela spotted Shoop and a man standing to the side, talking quietly. Another man, obviously a disc jockey, was seated behind a long console desk near the far wall that contained a computer, several telephones, and a large microphone. Behind the disc jockey were shelves of computer discs. The jockey wore headphones and was oblivious to—or ignoring Shoop and the man. Shoop motioned to Pamela to join him and she walked over to the two men.

"Dr. Barnes," he said, "this is the station manager, Roger Gallagher." Greetings were exchanged. "Mr. Gallagher, Dr. Barnes is assisting us with this investigation; she does acoustic analysis of sound and is analyzing the recording of Ballard's murder. She said she might need to ask you some questions and also, take some measurements in the studio if you don't mind..."

"No, of course not," replied Gallagher, "anything we can do. We want to find the person who did this."

"Mr. Gallagher," began Pamela, "several things. First, anything you can tell me about Ted Ballard—what type of person he was—his background—his friends—anything."

"That will be difficult," replied Gallagher, pushing up the sleeves of his sweater, "I hardly ever interacted with him. I was here at the station mostly during the day. Ted, as you know, had his show late on Saturday night—Sunday morning actually."

"Was he friends with anyone at the studio?"

"Not that I know," said Gallagher, "but you can ask Carl here when he gets a break. Their shifts overlapped."

"Dr. Barnes," interjected Shoop, "we've questioned all the disc jockeys about Ballard—his friends—and more specifically his enemies. I'll be glad to fill you in."

"Great," she said, "Mr. Gallagher, would it be possible to get another recording of Ballard? One from an earlier program possibly and not the night of the murder? I'd just like to compare his voice from one recording to another."

"No problem," answered Gallagher, "I'll go get one for you now. Something very early? When he first started perhaps?"

"That would be great," she said. Gallagher strode off through a wooden door in the far back wall, obviously happy to be out of there. At that moment, the disc jockey who had been reciting commercials and making on-air patter over the microphone, started playing a familiar Christmas song. The strains of the carol filled the studio and as Pamela looked over to the desk, the disc jockey removed his headset, rose, and ambled over to the twosome.

"Carl Edwards," he grinned, holding out his hand, "Nine to five. Almost done for the day."

"How do you do?" said Pamela, shaking his hand. Shoop greeted Edwards and asked if he would mind if they took a few measurements.

"Not a bit," said Edwards. "Measure away!"

"Have you thought of anything else, Mr. Edwards, about Ballard that you didn't mention when we interviewed you the other day?" asked Shoop.

"Could I sit at the console?" asked Pamela.

"Sure," replied Edwards to Pamela, "If you're game. I'm still freaked out a bit by sitting in that chair! Glad to have a few people around. Makes me feel safer." He sat in a chair against the wall and watched their efforts. Pamela brought out a small notebook and pen from her pocketbook and placed her jacket and purse on one of the chairs against the side wall. Then she began tabulating distances in the small studio. Shoop brought out a roll-up tape measure and helped her record the distance from microphone to desktop, desktop to door, and various other measurements. Pamela not only observed the actual numbers of each distance, but she also recorded a mental picture of the studio, the disc jockey's desk, the microphone, and everything in its vicinity.

"You know, Detective," said Edwards as he waited while the song he had introduced on air played over the intercom, "now that I'm thinking about Ted, I remember that he had just got a haircut."

"You noticed he got his hair cut?" asked Shoop, stopping in his assistant measuring duties.

"Yeah," replied Edwards from his chair by the window wall, "Ted was pretty scruffy—not that that makes any difference on air, but when he cleaned up, like getting an actual trim of all that long hair, I noticed. It didn't happen very often."

With the measurements completed, Pamela pulled out the disc jockey's chair and carefully sat down. Shoop wandered over to Edwards and continued questioning him about the haircut. The large, old-fashioned free-standing microphone before Pamela reminded her of a by-gone era. It was metal and the base was attached to the console. The microphone itself could be turned sideways and forward and backwards at the base. On its base in front was an on/off switch clearly labeled. To the right of the mic was a computer hard drive with four ports for CDs each labeled--#1 to #4. On the left of the console was a small switchboard with a landline phone. All around were piles of CDs and papers. Pamela reasoned that this was where the murder had occurred and she needed to be aware of each part of it. She measured distances from mic to floor and various other things she wanted to remember. When she believed she had all the data she might need—probably much more than she would need, she had Shoop roll up the tape and she tucked her small notebook in her purse. The station manager Gallagher returned through the door in the back wall, obviously a storage room.

"I found several of Ted's early shows," he said, wiping dust off the plastic covers of some hand-labeled CD's and handing them to Pamela.

"Thank you," she said, "I'll make copies and get these back..."

"Don't bother," said Gallagher, wiping his hands and smiling. "I have no use for them now."

"If you insist," Pamela replied, tucking the CD's into her pocketbook and slipping her jacket back on. "I believe that's all I need...."

"I'll walk you to your car," said Shoop, grabbing his coat. The two turned to go, leaving Gallagher and Edwards alone in the studio. As Shoop escorted Pamela out the front door of the little station, he stopped briefly, hands in pockets, wind blowing in the darkening sky.

"Dr. Barnes," he said, "I certainly hope you can help us. I just got the preliminary autopsy report on Mr. Ballard and there's very little information to go on."

"The autopsy report?" she asked.

"Pretty much what we already knew," he said, cringing as the wind pummeled his face. "One shot to the head with a handgun—a 38 caliber revolver. Unfortunately, no trace evidence of our killer at all. He evidently just walked in the door, shot Ballard, and left—never to be seen again."

"That's all you have?"

"Seems Ballard had no enemies. He actually had no friends either—some acquaintances, but no one with whom he was close. Oh, lots of people knew him—or knew of him. At least, they knew of his alter-ego—this Black Vulture, but Ted Ballard, lowly doctoral student in English—not so much. Can't imagine why anyone would want to kill him."

"Then, maybe," she said, "what I have might be helpful."

"What?" he asked, turning to look at her with anticipation.

"I believe I have found—or we have found—my colleague Willard Swinton and I—think we hear another voice on the murder tape. It appears to overlap Ballard's voice—softly from a distance. About the time the murder weapon would have been exposed—like an "ah" or "oh" or some sort of gasp."

"No words?"

"No, unfortunately, no 'I'm going to shoot you, Ballard' sort of confession," she sighed.

"That's better than anything we've got so far."

"We're working on analyzing this segment now. I really don't want to make any definitive claims but we suspect that it's male—probably from the south. I know, that's not much. I suppose most killers who use handguns are male and most people who kill people in the south probably are from the south themselves."

"It's still better than I had an hour ago," he said, nodding. "Thanks. Keep me updated on your work, Dr. Barnes."

"I will, Detective," she said, "but please, let's just keep this between the two of us. My husband doesn't really need to know, does he?"

"Just consider yourself a consultant," he replied, smiling and headed for his car.

"A consultant?" she said to herself, as she quickly climbed into her Civic. "I wonder if the Reardon Police Department would consider paying me consulting fees?"

Chapter 16

Previous week--Friday, December 14

"Daniel," the old man whispered, his voice dry and halting, "is that you?"

"Yes, father," replied Daniel, sitting on his father's bed, clutching the old gaunt hands, "I'm here."

"How is the plant?"

Daniel laughed and placed his palm on Charles Bridgewater's wrinkled cheek. "Leave it to you, Father, to be worrying about business. If you must know, I single-handedly repaired one of the old looms the other day. I climbed up to the top and yanked out a piece of stuck carpet. It's working fine now."

"Way to go, Tarzan," sputtered Charles, patting Daniel's other hand.

"You should be concentrating on getting better," said Daniel, squeezing the old man's hands with his own.

"I am," replied Charles, "I am better—much better now that you're here." He nodded in emphasis. Then slowly his eyes lost focus and his lids began to close.

"Yes, get some sleep," whispered Daniel in his ear as he placed the wizened hands on the old man's chest and pulled the coverlet up under his chin. He could see that his father was breathing steadily but weakly. With a sigh, he rose and turned towards the bedroom door. Upon exiting, he turned and gently pulled the large oaken door shut as silently as possible. When he turned towards the hallway, he found his father's nurse, Katherine, sitting patiently on a chair near the bedroom door, an embroidery hoop occupying her hands.

"He's sleeping, Katherine," Daniel reported to the woman, "Is Dr. Knowles around?"

"Yes, sir," she replied, "He's waiting for you in the kitchen."

"The kitchen?"

"I believe he wanted some coffee, sir," she said, rising with a polite bow, and quickly entered the old man's bedroom.

Daniel followed her exit with his eyes and when he turned around, he saw Dr. Knowles striding down the hallway, mug of coffee in one hand and his doctor's bag in the other.

"Daniel," announced Knowles as he neared the young man, "glad I caught you before you headed over to the plant." He took a quick sip from the mug and set down his case at his feet. "I know you like to keep updated."

"I do," replied Daniel, "How's he doing, Doctor?"

"Truthfully," answered Knowles, "about the same. Actually, I had expected greater decline. Usually in these cases, the decline is fairly steady—often rapid, but your father is holding his own. I don't know whether to upgrade his condition, keep it the same—or what? It's mystifying."

"A good mystery—as far as I'm concerned," said Daniel, "I don't suppose you would consider the possibility of a recovery?"

"Unlikely, I'm sorry to say," said Knowles, "About all we can hope for is more time. He's weak, but lucid. Often, you don't even have that."

Daniel restrained a soft smile, "He even was joking with me about the plant."

"A good sign," said Knowles, taking another sip from his mug.

"Doctor," said Daniel, taking a deep breath and placing his hand on the man's shoulder, "I need to take a trip, but I don't want to upset father. I'd probably be gone a few days. Do you think that would be advisable given his condition?"

"Truthfully, Daniel," said Knowles, facing the younger man directly, "I'm not sure if he even has a full awareness of time. He probably wouldn't even realize you were gone. I certainly wouldn't mention your intention to leave because that would probably upset him more than your not being here."

"That's what I was thinking," said Daniel, nodding. "I plan to leave today and hope to return in a few days."

"We can cover for you if he becomes agitated," said the doctor. "We'll just tell him you were just here and he forgot. In all likelihood, that will suffice."

"Good," Daniel said, grabbing the man's hand and shaking it profusely. "Thank you, Doctor. I'm counting on you to take good care of him while I'm gone."

"He is my top priority, Daniel," replied Knowles. They shook hands and Daniel grabbed his outer coat from a side table and headed down the hallway.

"Bernice," he spoke into his iPhone that was in the pocket of his overcoat, "contact Harold and have him meet me at the house." He continued down the long paneled hallway and turned at the end into a different wing of the large mansion. At the end of the new wing, he entered a large bedroom, decorated in a more modern style. He placed his overcoat on the king-sized bed and went to a large walk-in closet where he returned with a modern, navy and red suitcase with collapsible wheels and handle. He opened the case and placed it on the bed. Then he began opening drawers and closets and selecting items of clothing. Within a few minutes, he had filled the suitcase with several days worth of clothes, toiletries, and underwear—enough for a short trip. With this task complete, he closed the suitcase, set it on the floor and extended the handle. Putting on his overcoat and heading for the door, he pulled out his iPhone and again rang Bernice.

"Did you get a hold of Harold?"

"Yes, sir," she replied, "He's on his way. He'll meet you at the house."

"Good." He was tucking his iPhone back in his coat pocket as he strode down the long hallway that led back to the central foyer on the second floor. As he was heading down the mansion's beautiful central staircase, he saw the lawyer's car pull up to the front of the house through the tall glass windows on either side of the huge entrance doors.

Vickers parked his BMW immediately behind Daniel's Acura. It was incongruous, Daniel realized, that his lawyer's car was so much more luxurious than his own. But, Daniel far preferred his little Acura. He pulled his luggage through the main door and greeted Harold between their two cars.

"You taking a trip?" asked Vickers as he saw Daniel dragging the suitcase.

"Just a short one," replied Daniel as he unlocked his trunk and flung his luggage inside. Then, slamming down the trunk lid, he leaned against the back of his car. "Harold, I'm going to let you in on a secret."

"Great," said Vickers, pulling a wool scarf tighter around his neck, "Is it juicy?"

"I don't know what you'd consider juicy," replied Daniel, "and I don't know if you'll approve of what I'm going to do, but someone needs to know what I'm about to do and where I'm going. I figure it had better be you."

"Thanks," replied Vickers, "I hope you don't plan to get in any trouble, and implicate me, Daniel." The older man leaned against the front bumper of his BMW and folded his arms with a slight sneer.

"I hope not," said Daniel. "Jax found David." He waited as the news sunk in.

"My god," replied Vickers, his mouth and head jutting forward in disbelief, "where?"

"Not all that far actually," said Daniel, "he's been using an alias."

"Why?"

"He obviously didn't want to be found."

"And you're going to go visit him?" Vickers' face and voice showed his bewilderment.

"I'm going to try to bring him back," said Daniel, setting his chin in a determined rock-like firmness. "Hopefully, before father dies."

"Let me get this straight. David doesn't want to see Charles and Charles surely doesn't want to see him. So, you're going to try to bring them together."

"Sometimes you have to force people to do what's best for them." Daniel shrugged dramatically.

"This does not sound like a good idea, Daniel. In fact, it sounds potentially dangerous—at least unproductive. I wish you'd reconsider." Vickers placed his hand on the young man's arm and looked directly into his eyes. Harold was like an uncle to Daniel; he was certainly more than merely the family's attorney. Daniel had received and followed much of his advice.

"Harold, you've always gone along with father on ostracizing David, but I always felt that you never liked the idea."

"I'd like to see him return, of course," said Vickers, "on his own, preferably. But Daniel, there's a great deal of animosity between David and your father. All that agony over your mother—and her death. There was never any satisfactory closure about that. For all you know, even if you find David, he'll still be horribly resentful."

"I know," said Daniel, "but I hope I can overcome his doubts and bring him home. I have to try, Harold. I have to—for father."

"All right, I get it. I'm not thrilled, but I get it," said Harold. "Can you tell me where you're going?"

"A little town called Reardon—across the state line to the west. David's working on a graduate degree at the university there."

"That sounds good," said Vickers, "he was always very studious."

"Yes," said Daniel, "far too studious for father."

"I wish you luck, then." Vickers rose from the hood of his BMW and readied to go.

"One more thing," said Daniel, holding up a hand and pulling a white envelope from his inside jacket pocket. "I need to show you something. I guess now's as good a time as any—just don't freak out, please."

"Now what?" asked Vickers. He opened the envelope and brought out a legal document folded in thirds. He unfolded the paper and read the particulars quickly from top to bottom. "Oh, my god!"

"Yes, I figured you say that," said Daniel. "I'd like you to hold on to this while I'm gone—but don't show it or mention it to anyone—particularly father--for obvious reasons. I intend to make this all public quite soon, but I'd prefer to wait until after I have David and father reunited."

"Daniel, I don't know what to say," said Vickers, shaking his head, "I didn't think anyone could surprise me, but you certainly have. And don't worry. Your secret is safe with me. Have a good trip." He shook Daniel's hand and walked him to the driver's door of his Acura. "A safe trip." Daniel got into his car and drove out the circular drive of his family home, waving at Vickers as he departed.

As he pulled into the street, he pulled out his cell phone again. "Hey."

"Hey, yourself," said Amy Shuster, answering.

"Still at work?"

"Yes, but not terribly busy. Where are you?"

"Going to drop by for a minute, if that's okay?"

"I'm pouring your coffee now and cutting your pie," she said. Daniel drove with a sense of lightheartedness he hadn't felt in ages. Every day he thought of David. Every day he wondered about why his brother had left and why he didn't return. It all had happened some time after David's graduation from Dexter Military Academy. David was in the car with their mother, Elinore Bridgewater. There had been that terrible accident. Elinore was killed and David survived. Daniel always thought that maybe David felt guilty about Elinore's death and that's why he left—or Charles Bridgewater was so heartbroken about his wife's death and maybe blamed David because he was in the car—that he threatened him or scared him away. Daniel was never really sure—neither his father nor David ever said. One day, David was gone and Charles never made any attempt to find him and told Daniel to forget him. Now, with Charles sick, Daniel was in the driver's seat. Here was his chance to find out what had happened that terrible day. Here was his chance to put an end to the suffering of the people involved. He knew his father had to miss David— had to feel guilty for sending him away—or at least for not trying to get him to stay. David must surely feel guilty for remaining away for all these years.

He pulled into the concrete lot of Sam's Diner. He could see through the glass front of the diner that the place was virtually deserted—as it usually was late in the afternoon after the lunch crowd and before the supper crowd. Amy was usually the only waitress on duty at this time. This was actually how they had met because he often didn't find time for a meal until halfway through the afternoon. Amy was a good listener—a great listener—and she had never treated him like the CEO of Compton's biggest employer. She had treated him like a nice guy—which he was. Their afternoon chats became longer and more frequent and soon Daniel was a regular at Sam's Diner and in Amy's heart.

He entered the premises and waved at the cashier, a non-talkative gum chewer who was draped over the cash register reading the latest *People* magazine. She gave him her regular greeting—an eye roll—and he sauntered down the long aisle between the counter and the one row of booths flush against the front windows. He settled in at the last booth—for more privacy--and Amy appeared out of the kitchen door with her cup of coffee and promised pie. She placed the cup and the pie in front of him and sat down on the other side of the booth.

"I dropped by to say good-bye," he announced, grabbing her hands. They were warm; his were cold.

"Good-bye?" she said, startled, "where are you going?"

"We found David," he whispered with enthusiasm.

"Oh, Dan," she replied, squeezing his hands, "that's wonderful! Does he know you're coming?"

"Nope," he said, squishing his shoulders and face together in anticipation of her fury. "Don't hit me." He tore into the peach pie between sips of coffee.

"You're just going to descend on him?" she asked incredulous.

"I'm afraid he might run away if I don't."

"Dan, this is crazy!" She grabbed his arms and gesticulated furiously.

"I've got to do it—I've got to convince him to return and make amends with father before he dies."

"Can't that Jax fellow—the investigator--do this?" Her blonde bangs refused to hold still on her animated face.

"No, I have to do it. Jax found him, but I have to be the one to confront him."

"Then, I'm going with you," she said, starting to gather her belongings. He grabbed and pulled her back into the booth.

"No," he said firmly. "Amy, no. I need to do this alone. Sweet, we're almost there. Almost where we want to be—no more secrets. As soon as I straighten out this feud between David and father—then I can concentrate on us. I promise." He scraped his fork over the bottom of the small plate and licked the last bit of peach filling from it.

"I trust you, Dan," she said, looking sadly into his eyes. "It's not a question of me being anxious to—to—I just worry about you. I just don't think you should do this all by yourself." She touched his hair with her hand and slowly brushed it back.

"Oh, for heaven's sake," he laughed, "I just repaired a defective loom with a pair of pliers and my teeth. I can handle a short trip to visit the wayward David."

"You're determined?" she asked, now sitting straight, her hands clasped together in front of her.

"I'm leaving now. Just stopped by to kiss you good-bye."

"You'd better do it quickly," she smiled, benignly, "Cherry has the magazine in front of her face, but she'll turn a page any minute." He bent over the table and softly placed his lips against her. "Perfect lips," he announced. "They go well with peach pie." He smiled at her and stood up.

"Dan," she said, as he pulled on his coat. He turned.

"I love you," she mouthed the words.

"I love you too," he repeated the silent message, pointing to his heart and to hers. Then he turned and disappeared out of the diner.

Chapter 17

Present time--Tuesday morning, December 18

"Dr. Barnes," called out Jane Marie, as Pamela entered the main office to pick up her mail from her cubby hole. Pamela stepped into the secretary's alcove and tipped her head expectantly to the young woman's words. "Dr. Barnes, what are you up to?" She pointed another candy cane at Pamela and shook it at her. The small nook that was Jane Marie's office was a veritable wonderland of Christmas decorations.

"Me?" asked Pamela with a start, clutching her papers, books, and now mail to her chest.

"You were in with Dr. Marks for quite a while yesterday," continued Jane Marie, a sprig of holly in her silky brown curls bouncing as she gestured authoritatively towards Pamela, "and after you left, I heard him playing a recording of that disc jockey that was murdered." She stopped briefly when she said 'murdered' and quickly looked around, "at KRDN Saturday night. Now why would he be doing that?" Her nostrils flared and her eyes expanded as she waited for Pamela to provide answers. A plastic reindeer played 'Rudolph' in the background."

"It's no big secret, Jane Marie," said Pamela. Actually, she and Jane Marie had shared a number of secrets over the years. Jane Marie kept her informed of some of the best—and juiciest—departmental gossip. She was in the perfect location to hear and observe all the comings and goings of everyone. "I gave Mitchell a CD of the murder to see if he might provide some information about the gun that was used. And before you ask, Detective Shoop gave me the original CD; it's not a secret—anyone who happened to be listening to KRDN Saturday night would have heard the same thing."

"So, you're in the detecting business again, are you, Dr. Barnes?"

"Not full-time, Jane Marie," replied Pamela, turning to go, "just as a side line. I promise I won't neglect my departmental duties." She grabbed a cookie from the tray of Christmas goodies Jane Marie had on her desk and gobbled it down. Gym tonight, for sure, she thought.

"I'll be checking up on you," replied the secretary, again shaking her pencil at the teacher and smiling. Pamela headed out of the alcove, nibbling on the goodie, and immediately bumped into her colleague Bob Goodman, checking his mail.

"Bob," she greeted him, licking her finger tips, "Good morning!"

"Hmm," grumbled the tall professor as he bent low to peek into his mail box placed far below eye level.

"Problems?"

"You should know, Pamela," he responded, standing upright and turning to face her directly. My goodness, she thought, this was about as curt as Bob had ever been; he was usually gracious and thoughtful. "You and Joan seem to be egging Arliss on in your hen sessions over here."

"Our what?" Was this the real Bob Goodman? Or had Scrooge taken his place?

"I'm sorry, Pamela, if I seem insensitive (yes, you do! thought Pamela) but Arliss and I were working out our wedding situation and now---now—she's vacillating."

"You mean, she's changed her mind about marrying you?" Pamela asked, aghast. She thought she had never seen a couple more in sync—and in love—than Bob and Arliss.

"No, no," he said, gesturing wildly, "just the wedding. Good Lord, if it were just up to me it wouldn't matter, but my mother is---Pamela, you just don't know. This is a huge event to her. She's planning this mammoth soiree—and Arliss just refuses to get on board. She doesn't seem to care about a wedding at all! Does that seem normal to you?"

"No," said Pamela, carefully, because she knew that she would be hard pressed to describe anything Arliss MacGregor did as normal. "Bob, you must understand, that Joan and I are not—egging her on—as you put it—we're merely trying to support her. My understanding was that she wasn't even certain she wanted to get married at all. She said to us she was completely content with the way things are—you know—just living with you."

"Pamela," he said, folding his hands, and appearing to set forth a lecture that a father of a teenager might give to his child going out in the family car for the first time, "Arliss and I cannot continue to 'live together' indefinitely. Actually, no such living arrangement exists at all—if anyone were to ask." No, she'd change that to strict Puritan preacher giving a hellfire and brimstone sermon.

"Such as your mother?"

"I see you understand," he replied. Then, apparently completely lost in his dilemma, he grabbed his mail, shaking his head and wandered off down the opposite end of the main hallway towards the animal psychology wing.

"Strange," said Pamela, to herself and she too wandered off down the hallway the other way and up the side staircase to her office on the second floor.

When she reached her office door, she discovered three students sitting on the floor, leaning against the wall. She recognized two of them from her undergraduate research class and the third as Kent Drummond, her graduate assistant—and would-be suitor of her daughter. She smiled at the trio and quickly opened her door. Slipping inside, she hung up her jacket on her coat tree and set her brown paper bag and thermos on her desk with her purse. Then waving her arm for the students to enter, she sat at her desk.

"What can I do for you?" she asked. Kent motioned for the other two students to go first. They had quick questions about a homework assignment. Pamela answered them to the students' satisfaction and they were soon on their way. Kent remained.

"Hey, Dr. B," he said, sitting on the arm of her sofa, "I just brought you the survey data from the participants I collected yesterday in the lab." This was Kent's second year as her assistant and she dreaded the end of the academic year when he would—if all went well—receive his Master's degree and leave the program. Until then, she was blessed with one of the most industrious and conscientious laboratory assistants she'd ever had. In fact, he was usually a step ahead of her—anticipating situations before they became problems. The incongruity was that he looked like something out of a comic book—wild hair with purple spikes, all black clothing with strange, usually frightening designs—and, of course, the ubiquitous sneakers. Add to that the fact that he was dating her daughter—much to the chagrin of her husband—and Kent was an enigma.

"Can you go ahead and enter it?" she asked. "I don't really need to go over the data. If it's at all like last week's, we should be on the right track." Their present research study was almost complete; they almost had enough participants to start running their analysis. It would give her a lot to keep her busy over the Christmas holiday—hurray!

"Sure," he said, "no problem. I'll go get started on it." He turned to exit her office.

"Kent," she called to him, "Just curious. Did you have any more thoughts about that Ted Ballard…uh…Black Vulture? The murdered disc jockey?"

"I know who you mean, Dr. B," he said, leaning against her doorway. "I've seen him around at some of the local clubs—probably in New Orleans too. There are some great alternative music groups there---a lot of them underground."

"What do you mean underground?"

"Underground…I mean, not public. You find out about a band playing there pretty much by word of mouth."

"And you've been to these underground clubs?"

"Yeah," he replied, "some are pretty strange." She thought, they must be if Kent considered them strange. "Some of the members even believe themselves to be vampires."

"Vampires?"

"Not all, but there are some weirdoes in the alternative music scene. You know, Goth or emo. Depends on who you talk to what they call it."

"And you saw this Black Vulture at these clubs?"

"Pretty sure. Once or twice. I've seen him here in Reardon, too. Mostly at the Blue Poppy, like I told you."

"Did he have any friends?"

"Gee, Dr. B," he said, thinking and scrunching his face together so much that the spikes on his head tipped at a different odd angle. "I never heard anyone say they were close to him. Lot of people knew him—he was Black Vulture, you know."

"Yes, I know," she said.

"Hey, Dr. B," he said, looking at his watch, "I gotta get going. Got a class in a few minutes." He waved farewell and she waved briefly to him. She sat down at her desk and got ready for a long day of classes. This was Tuesday and her longest day of the week. She had her Tuesday night graduate seminar.

Hours later, after her morning classes, she sat in a booth at the Reardon Coffee Factory, in the center of the downtown area. She had arrived early and had grabbed one of their favorite locations off to the side. The front portion of The Factory housed the restaurant; the actual factory where the plants were prepared, roasted, and brewed into coffee substitutes was in the back. When you entered the old brick building through the ancient iron-grilled doors, you felt as if you were back in 1860. Wonderful aromas of—yes—coffee, but much more assaulted the senses. In the center of the restaurant's high beamed ceiling hung an ancient sign that looked like it might have been drawn by Romulus Reardon himself. It read, "You grow it; we brew it."

Almost as soon as she had slid into the darkened booth, Joan and Arliss appeared and slid in beside and across from her. Joan looked concerned and Arliss looked furious. Oh, no, she thought, now what is the latest catastrophe in the Bob Goodman—Arliss MacGregor romance? They both looked anxious to talk.

"What's wrong?" asked Pamela as she turned first from one friend to the other.

"Bob's mother!" cried Arliss.

"The poor dear," said Joan to Pamela, sympathetically, "the woman is the mother-in-law from hell!"

"What?" asked Pamela.

Before she could find out, their peppy young waitress appeared and took their order—fairly mundane sandwich and salad fare for all, but Pamela ordered sassafras coffee and Arliss selected dandelion coffee. Joan pondered the long list of alternate coffee choices before deciding on cottonseed coffee.

"Cottonseed!" exclaimed Arliss, "That's like drinking a shirt, isn't it?"

"You have no sense of adventure, Arliss," countered Joan.

"Stop it, you two," interjected Pamela, placing her body between her two friends. "What about Bob's mother?"

"She's insisting on a huge—a huge---ceremony in an Episcopalian cathedral!" moaned Arliss, beating her hands on the table.

"Is Bob Episcopalian?" asked Pamela.

"I suppose," said Arliss, "but Pamela, you should see this place—it's like where the Queen of England was crowned!"

"And what does Bob say about all this?"

"He doesn't care," said Arliss, "he's gone along with this woman all his life. He says 'It's just for a day—let's just put up with it!'"

"And I take it you don't want the huge ceremony in the giant cathedral?" asked Pamela, carefully.

"I want to elope," responded Arliss, "if we must get married—the simpler, the better. He should have never told this woman..."

"His mother?" asked Pamela, delicately. Was there a way to mediate this problem for Bob and Joan. She remembered how miserable Bob had looked this morning when she saw him at the mailboxes. She glanced to her side at Joan who gave her a shrug. Obviously, she had tried and failed and it was evidently Pamela's job now.

"That's not the worst of it!" shrieked Arliss, "She plans to get her personal designer to create a dress for me!"

"Would that be so horrible?" asked Pamela, thinking how much she wouldn't have minded having a couture wedding dress when she and Rocky got married.

"I prefer jeans!"

"Not for your wedding!" scolded Joan, interjecting her first comment since arriving. Obviously she was tired from arguing with Arliss already.

"Wedding—schmedding!" sneered Arliss. "It's my wedding, whatever it is! Bob's mother shouldn't be directing it!"

"No," agreed Pamela, "you and Bob should. Have you told him that?"

"He's a coward where his mother is concerned," said Arliss, her body sliding down into the leather bench and leaning against the wall.

"Really?" queried Pamela. "Bob has never struck me as a coward. He's probably one of the most principled individuals I know."

"Have you seen his mother? She looks like a flower-covered truck," cried Arliss. She was almost in tears. Pamela had never seen her friend so desolate.

Just then, the waitress arrived with their orders and the three women suspended discussion while they chewed and sipped.

"My dear," said Joan eventually, leaning across the table to Arliss, "I've told you this, and I'm sure Pamela will agree. We're happy to serve as sounding boards for you, but ultimately, you must talk honestly to Bob about this. He is your fiancé..." Arliss grimaced at Joan's use of the word 'fiancé' which she obviously did not consider herself. "He is your boyfriend...mate...future husband...whatever...and I know he considers you his equal. If you can't work together on this problem, how do you ever expect to solve problems once you're married?" Joan glanced knowingly over the tops of her reading glasses at Arliss, holding them firmly to her face.

"All right, all right," said Arliss, huffing. "Thank God, my parents are nothing like Bob's mother. They could care less when...where...how...or if I get married." She smiled smugly at her two friends.

"In the grand scheme of things," continued Joan, "so you wear a beautiful dress and let people gush over you for a few hours. Isn't it worth a little bit of discomfort to make Bob—and his mother—happy?" Oh, Joan, thought Pamela as she savored her cup of sassafras coffee, you diplomat. The horrible discomfort of a Vera Wang!

"I suppose," said Arliss, now totally deflated. "I'm still going to talk to him and try to talk him out of it."

"You do that, my dear," said Joan, reaching over the table and patting Arliss's hand. "Now, Pamela," she said, turning to her, "whatever happened yesterday after we left you alone with that strange detective?"

"Not much," said Pamela, lightly, stretching her arms out over the blue and white-covered tablecloth. "He just asked me to consult on the disc jockey murder."

"What?" yelled Arliss, completely forgetting her wedding blues.

"Yes," said Pamela, smiling and straightening her collar with pride, "seems he wants me to try to identify the killer from a recording of the murder."

"Just like you did with Charlotte?" asked Joan.

"Exactly," responded Pamela.

"So," said Arliss, her thin frame leaning over her sandwich platter, now totally involved in the conspiracy, "did you identify him?"

"Or her," said Pamela, "The killer used a gun. It could have been a woman."

"It could have," agreed Arliss. "It could have been Bob's mother!"

"But it was a man," said Pamela, cup to lips. "At least that's what Willard and I believe by listening to the recording. A southern man. We believe the killer actually spoke on the recording when he—or she—brought out the gun. It's hard to hear—but there's a soft "ah" sound and we've analyzed it and that's our best guess."

"A Southern man," said Joan, wiping a dab of mayonnaise from her upper lip, "describes half the population of Reardon."

"It's still better than what the police had on their own," said Pamela, her chest heaving as she defended her findings.

"True," said Arliss. "Pam, I bet you solve this murder just like you did Charlotte's."

"I'd like to. Of course, I can't tell Rocky," she added, clutching her cup with determination "He's far too protective."

"See!" screamed Arliss, "I'm not the only one arguing with their significant other."

"Yes, dear," agreed Joan, "but Pamela has learned how to circumvent her husband and his demands—not to confront him directly. You will learn too, eventually."

"True," agreed Pamela, "I'd like to circumvent Rocky and go down to that Blue Poppy."

"The blue what?" asked Arliss.

"The Blue Poppy," repeated Pamela. "It's a club downtown, a few blocks south of here, where they play a lot of this alternate music that that disc jockey Ted Ballard—I mean Black Vulture—played on his show. I'd like to talk to some people who maybe knew him or know about this type of music. I'd like to see if I could find out more about him—particularly who might have had it in for him."

"Pam," gasped Arliss, "surely, the police don't expect you to do that?"

"No," replied Pamela, "it's just something that I think would help give me some background material to make my acoustic analysis easier—like research."

"Yes," said Joan, folding her napkin neatly and placing it beside her plate. She smiled sedately, "I know what you mean, my dear. You need to conduct some research. Well, we're all three researchers, aren't we? Why don't the three of us check out this Blue Poppy? How much different can it be from our regular girls' night out haunt—*Who-Who's?*"

"Oh, Joan," exclaimed Arliss, "that sounds like a great idea! Pam, let's go researching!"

"I can't go tonight; I have my graduate seminar," she replied, "but tomorrow night might work. Can you both make it tomorrow?"

"My nights are free!" said Joan "I'm the merry widow!"

"Mine too!" agreed Arliss, "It will give me a break from wedding planning!"

Chapter 18

Previous week--Friday evening, December 14

Daniel found himself driving on back highways—something he usually didn't do. It turned out that Reardon was directly west of the Bridgewater factory in Compton—probably around 200 miles as the crow flies. Unfortunately, there were no direct routes and certainly no Interstate. When he entered Reardon into his GPS navigational system on the dashboard of his Acura, the map that popped up—purportedly the shortest distance—showed a winding snake-like curved line. All the roads he noticed were small state— or worse-- county roads.

Now, it was early evening around five o'clock he realized as he checked his watch, but mid-December made it seem more like nine o'clock. The scenery here was pleasant— he'd seen pheasants and lots of woodland creatures zip across the road as he turned the many curves, probably an indication of how few actual vehicles took these back roads. Keeping his eyes on the road ahead, he briefly glanced down at his on-board map. There were precious few towns between here and Reardon he realized. Normally, he would never talk on his iPhone while driving—he was a stickler for obeying the law, but the road was virtually deserted and he was carefully watching his speed because he'd heard about speed traps in locations just such as these.

"Hey," he spoke into the cell when Amy answered on the first ring. "I'm looking at a beautiful sunset and thinking of you."

"I appreciate poetry," she replied, "but I'd rather have you pay attention to your driving."

"It's calm," he said, "no traffic to speak of. It's just taking me longer than I anticipated. These are really winding roads and I ran into a lot of construction about an hour back."

"You don't think you'll make Reardon tonight?"

"I'm thinking maybe I should stop," he agreed, "It's getting dark and I've got over 100 miles left. It might be better to make my appearance at David's doorstep when I'm fresh—and when he's fresh. Tomorrow. Besides, he might be in class today—he is a student."

"But not late on a Friday night," she suggested.

"No," he agreed, "I guess I'm just exhausted and probably putting off the inevitable."

"You could come home," she said, with a slight pleading note. He knew she wasn't thrilled about this trip.

"It'll be all right," he assured her. "I'm thinking I may stop for the night, get some supper and a good night's sleep and then I can arrive early tomorrow and go straight to his apartment. You know, catch him before he leaves for the day."

"If he leaves," she said, "Maybe he sleeps late. You said his radio program was Saturday night, didn't you?"

"Yes," he answered, seeing her wheels turning as she helped him plan the best approach to the long-lost David. "He might sleep late. Even so, I think tomorrow morning is the best time. Besides, I'm beat and driving on these winding roads is much worse than driving on the Interstate."

She laughed. "Okay," she said, "but good luck finding anyplace to eat as good as Sam's."

"Sweet," he sighed, "there's no place as good as Sam's. I'll just have to make do." They laughed together and he added, "I probably should tell you that I told Harold about our situation."

"You did?"

"He's very discreet," Daniel explained, "but I wanted you to know in case you should need anything—you can go to him."

"I'll be fine," she assured him. "Do you want me to Google good restaurants in your location?"

"Nah," he chuckled, "I can rough it. Besides, remember, I have the GPS. It does restaurant and hotel locating as well. I'll give it a workout in just a bit."

"Oh, technology," she exclaimed. "If only you could GPS me a kiss."

"No way," he pouted, "I don't want some keyboard getting between my lips and yours. Anyway, I'd better get going—it's really starting to get dark and I've got to concentrate."

"Okay," she said, "Love you."

"Love you, too." He clicked off their conversation and replaced his iPhone in his jacket pocket. Poking around on his GPS, he hit the button to search for nearby hotels and restaurants and discovered that he was nearing a town on the state border. The device indicated a host of several hotels and motels and accompanying eateries. Great, he thought. I'd better stop here, because I have no idea if I'll find anything better between here and Reardon.

As he reached the top of a small hill, he could see lights flickering in the distance. Several large colorful signs stood out and several billboards proclaimed the wonders of an upcoming inn. Hmm, he thought. That one looks clean and presentable—hotel and food. Let's see if there are any vacancies. He guided his GPS cursor to the spot where the multitude of small red dots clumped. The advertised hotel popped up—Green Forest Inn. He pulled out his iPhone again and tapped in the number of the inn. Within a few minutes, Daniel had booked himself a room in the cozy-looking place and extracted directions from the pleasant sounding desk clerk. Evidently, not many people chose to stay at the Green Forest Inn, in the middle of nowhere, a week before Christmas.

He drove a few miles further down the far side of the hill and followed the next two or three billboards which gave excellent directions (actually better than those of the desk clerk) to the inn. As he maneuvered his Acura up a small and winding trail, following the arrows, clearly labeled "Green Forest Inn" he soon discovered himself in front of a large white mansion with an expansive front porch, green shutters and a large green door with one of those old-fashioned brass knockers. Several cars were parked in front, so the Green Forest Inn wasn't as out of the way as he thought. He gave it a brief rap and it was immediately opened by a young woman who welcomed him into a warm, wood-paneled lobby. He could see a dining room in the distance where a fire crackled in the fireplace. The aroma of home-cooked food wafted from the direction of the room. It smelled wonderful, he realized, though, of course, not as wonderful as Sam's. As luck would have it, he was able to get a room and after a filling and delicious dinner in the Christmas-decorated dining room, he returned to his room and plopped down on a bouncy four poster bed with an extremely soft, even plusher comforter.

If he were not on such an important task, he might actually enjoy this wonderful little inn. He certainly wished that Amy were here with him. She loved traditional places like this with home-style decorating. She'd probably want to sit in the dining room in front of the beautiful stone fireplace and drink mulled wine. Not a bad idea, he thought, with a sigh. Too bad. He decided he'd better forego all thoughts of enjoying himself and get to bed promptly so he could get up as early as possible. He had a big day tomorrow and he wanted to get on the road early. If he left here by six he could probably be in Reardon by nine. That should be early enough, he thought.

He sprawled across the old bed and sank down into the springs. Just a few more hours and he'd be face to face with David. So many years. What would he be like? How would he have changed? He knew he'd recognize him. But, what he was like now? Why had he disappeared and never contacted them since? It was a mystery—one he hoped would soon be solved. He fell asleep—but he did not sleep soundly.

Chapter 19

Present time--Tuesday evening, December 18

Pamela's graduate acoustics seminar was finishing up a successful semester. She felt lucky that she had seven such excellent students and future researchers in her class. They were all enthusiastic and intelligent and stimulating; her Tuesday nights were never boring. Tonight they had met in the computer lab rather than the seminar room so they could try out some of the new acoustic software available for sound analysis that Pamela believed they needed to have in their repertoire. She was standing at the front of the lab, behind the master console (where she had first detected the recording of Charlotte Clark's murder that was made inadvertently while Charlotte was being strangled). On the overhead screen she demonstrated a filtering technique that could be used to discriminate various sounds from others on a recording—something she had just used to extract that small bit of sound that she believed was the voice of the murderer on the recording of the killing of the disc jockey.

"Dr. Barnes,' said one of students, a male—pointing to his computer screen which displayed the same perspective as that on the overhead, "I understand how to filter, I'm just not certain how we would determine when to filter out a segment?"

"Paul," she said, smiling at the young man, "I'm afraid that decision is a judgment call. There are so many instances where you're going to have to try different things—many of which won't work. You'll just have to go with your gut."

"That doesn't sound very scientific," said one girl with a friendly leer.

"It doesn't, does it?" she laughed with the class.

"Dr. Barnes," continued the first young man with the filtering concern, "I guess my underlying problem is I can't put any of this in context. I just don't see how it would function in a real world situation."

"Real world?" asked Pamela.

"You know," Paul explained, "such as, where would I ever use this filtering protocol?"

"Hmm," she said, tapping her fingers on the console desk and looking around as if she expected a spy to appear from nowhere. "Real world? Did any of you hear about the murder of the local disc jockey at KRDN on Saturday night?"

The class looked around at each other, mumbling and nodding that most of them had heard of it. Some admitted that they had actually been listening when the murder itself took place.

"So, you would consider the disc jockey—his name was Ted Ballard..."

"Black Vulture," added one somber-looking dark-haired young woman in the second row of computers.

"Yes," continued Pamela, "Black Vulture. A real world problem. Either way, this murder was recorded. It took place at a radio station and the station automatically records all programs—including anything their on-air talent says."

"So, Dr. Barnes," asked another girl in the front row, "do you have a recording of the murder?"

"I do, Ellen," she responded, and grabbed her pocket book, which was on the console, opened it, and drew out a CD in a plastic container. "Would you like to see if you can analyze the acoustic output?"

The students all answered in enthusiastic agreement as Pamela entered the CD into the master console, where immediately on the overhead screen and simultaneously at each computer, appeared the wavy and jerky line of the recording in the sound analysis software they had been using in the course. Pamela placed her cursor on the spot on the line that she knew would include the last few moments of the recording and hit the play button. The familiar voice of Ted Ballard, alias Black Vulture, boomed from the overhead speakers and from each student's computer speaker. All heads were riveted to their screens as the unseen murder played out while the cursor raced horizontally over the wavy line and ended abruptly with the gun shot—then a few seconds and then the sound ended.

They all looked up. It was as if they had just witnessed a murder and for a moment, no one could speak. Then suddenly, everyone seemed to have ideas and questions. Pamela anticipated this.

"Dr. Barnes," said the enthusiastic Ellen in the front row, "there's another speaker! Right there after the disc jockey says....look! There's two lines! You can see them!"

"Yes!" agreed a tall boy in the second row, "the second voice is softer but you can definitely hear it. That must be the murderer!"

"Okay," said Pamela to her excited class, holding her hands up to calm them all down. "Yes, there is a second voice—Dr. Swinton and I discovered it yesterday and reported it to the police. We even analyzed the voice and believe it to be male and Southern."

"That's great!" said a girl with glasses. "Does that help the police, Dr. Barnes?"

"I don't know," answered Pamela. "I'm just trying to go over this tape and report whatever I find—let's say report whatever we find. There's no reason why you all can't participate in this analysis. Your eyes and ears are just as good as mine on this. I may have more experience, but with something like this—all the minds we have working on it, the more likely we are to find something." She smiled warmly at them and turned and replayed the brief segment again—and then a third time. The students listened carefully and watched the acoustic line as it played out in real time.

"Any other ideas about what you're seeing or hearing?" she asked.

"Dr. Barnes," said a red-haired girl in the back row, skeptically, "I'm not really sure this is the kind of thing you're looking for, but how does the tape end? After the gunshot? It seems to end because the recording ends—

someone turns off the microphone or the recording a few seconds after the shot."

"Yes, Polly," Pamela said, "I see that. What are you getting at?"

"My question is," the girl continued, "'Who turned the recording off?' I mean, the victim was the disc jockey and he was at the mic, but he didn't turn the mic off—he was dead. The killer was at the door, right? Why would he have walked over and turned off the mic or pulled the plug? I mean, I would think the killer would just leave and the recording would keep playing until the police or the station manager showed up and found the body."

"It's a very good question, Polly," said Pamela. "I will definitely discuss it with Detective Shoop."

"Are you helping with the investigation, Dr. Barnes?" asked another student.

"Only to provide insight into the recording," she said, "Actually, anyone who was listening to the program Saturday night could have heard the murder. Anyone might have a recording of it." She felt it necessary she realized to justify the fact that she had discussed the recording now with not only several colleagues but an entire class of students too.

"Anything else?" she asked her class.

"It's strange, Dr. Barnes," said the young man, Paul, who had started this conversation in the first place, "that the murderer doesn't say anything—oh, I know, he says something, but it sounds more like a gasp—like he's shocked—not like he's about to kill someone."

"I would be shocked if I was about to kill someone!" declared Ellen.

"But," continued Paul, "you'd think a killer would say something like, "I hate you, you bastard, and I'm going to kill you!"

"Not," interjected Ellen, "if he was killing a disc jockey speaking into a microphone. He'd know it would be heard by the audience."

"So, why didn't he wait until music was playing? Why did he kill him while the disc jockey was talking? It seems potentially more dangerous to kill him then, doesn't it?" argued Paul.

"Yeah," agreed another student, "unless he intentionally did it while this Ballard was on air so people would hear the killing."

"Why would he do that?" questioned another.

"Dr. Barnes," asked a quiet girl in the back, "do the police know if the disc jockey had any enemies?"

"As far as I know, they know of no enemies," declared Pamela, "but the investigation is still on-going."

"Another thing, Dr. Barnes," said another young man, "Ballard gets in quite a bit of information from the time the killer enters until the gun shot—but when you think about it—none of it helps identify the killer. There is something that seems obvious to me though from what Ballard says."

"What?" demanded a number of the students.

"Ballard didn't know the killer," he responded, "If he had known the killer, surely, he would have greeted him by name. But he doesn't. He asks him if he's a fan? Why he's there? And when the killer brings out the gun, Ballard doesn't say anything that would indicate that he knows why he's going to be killed, such as 'I'm sorry' or 'I didn't mean it' so I think he's totally in the dark as to who his killer is and why he's killed."

"Does that mean that you think this is some random killing?" one of the girls asked Pamela.

"I don't know, Teri," said Pamela. "The police don't seem to think it's random. The radio station was an out of the way place. Ballard was the only one there. This has all the marks, they say, of an intentional killing."

"But why?" asked a male student in the back row.

"And who?" said Pamela, "That's our job to find out. Let's get back to work." The class continued reviewing the recording until the end of class. At that time, Pamela made duplicate copies of the murder recording for each of them and asked them to keep studying it on their own. Then she dismissed the class and headed home.

When she arrived home, Rocky was waiting for her at the kitchen door.

"You had a phone call," he said, looking perturbed, his arms tightly folded.

"Who?" she asked.

"Your old favorite Detective Shoop," he said, "He wanted to know if you'd made any headway in analyzing the murder tape?" Rocky emphasized the word 'murder' and glared at her.

"Now, Rocky," she said, cringing, "I did not butt my nose into this like you're probably thinking. Shoop came to my office...."

"Which you evidently weren't ever going to tell me?"

"I knew it would just make you mad."

"And keeping me from being mad is far more important than getting yourself involved in another murder investigation? You were almost killed by that maniac last year!"

"Rocky, Rocky," she sighed. "Please." She threw her head back and slumped into a kitchen chair. "I can't, just can't do this now. I am totally exhausted."

"Then, go to bed," he said, huffing and storming off into the living room, "I won't keep you awake! I'll sleep on the couch!" He went to the linen closet at the end of the hallway and pulled out a blanket and a pillow and returned to the living room where he flung himself and the linens on the sofa, turning his back to her.

She grabbed her belongings and walked to the bedroom, every muscle aching. Never in their twenty-two years of marriage had Rocky refused to sleep with her. She got ready for bed and crawled under the covers. Tears dotted her cheeks. She was so tired, but how could she sleep with Rocky mad at her?

Chapter 20

Previous week--Saturday morning, December 15

Finding his way to David's small apartment had been relatively easy. David lived in a small brick complex off a tree-lined residential street situated about midway between downtown Reardon and campus. The building was set at a 90 degree angle to the street and parking slots separated the driveway from the building. All of the apartments had outside entrances. David's was a second story unit, so Daniel had to climb a flight of stairs located about half-way down the building and then backtrack a few units to get to David's—204. He had parked his Acura in the only "visitor" slot available and left his suitcase in the trunk. He hadn't planned any further than this meeting and didn't know if he'd be staying here, at a hotel, or turning around immediately and going home.

The wind picked up as he knocked on the thin, bent metal screen door. There was no bell that he could see. The sound was weak and he doubted anyone inside could hear it, so he knocked again—harder. From inside, further back in the apartment, a voice called out, "All right, I'm coming. Keep your pants on." The door was jerked open and a man appeared behind the screen of the metal door. His hair was a bit longer than Daniel's and puffed up and messy. He was unshaven and looked as if he'd been recently awakened—but even so, there was no doubt that this was David Bridgewater.

"Hey, David," said Daniel, smiling and shivering in the increasing wind, "long time no see."

"What are you doing here?" retorted David after a few seconds pause, yawning and scowling.

"Visiting my long lost brother," replied Daniel, bouncing up and down on his feet, "Could I come in or are you going to make me stand out here freezing my ass off?"

"How'd you find me?"

"I'll be happy to explain everything, really," said Daniel, "if I could just come in?"

David Bridgewater leaned his forehead against the screen door, staring intently at the man on the other side. Finally, he abruptly ripped open the screen door and allowed Daniel to enter the small, dark apartment. Inside, Daniel found himself in a living room—at least the appearance of a couch and recliner indicated as much. A tiny kitchen was visible across a counter that separated the living room from the kitchen-dining room area. The couch was covered with an old printed blanket that had seen better days but was probably in place to cover even worse markings on the sofa. There were several dilapidated end tables and a few mismatched lamps—none of which were turned on. The whole place was dark because all the curtains were closed. The kitchen counter was strewn with pizza boxes and empty beer cans and the smell of trash permeated the tiny apartment.

"What d'ya want?" asked David, standing directly in front of Daniel, still in confrontational mode.

"Could I sit down?" asked Daniel, "I've been driving quite a ways to get here."

"Not at my request," said David, but he pointed at the couch where Daniel walked to and gingerly checking the safely of the inner springs by first testing the cushions with his hand, finally sat carefully on the edge.

"I repeat," said David, still standing in the center of the room, "what do you want?"

"I want to find my brother—you," said Daniel, "is that a crime?"

There was a long pause as David stared at Daniel. He walked to the door and closed it and then walked to the recliner and sat down. "He sent you, didn't he?"

"If you mean Father," said Daniel, "the answer is 'no.' He doesn't even know I'm here."

"That's unlikely," said David, "he knows everything."

"Not now, David," Daniel said softly, leaning towards his brother across the room, "he's sick—in fact, he's dying."

"Really?" said David, with a disbelieving smile. "You expect me to believe that."

"Why not? It's true."

"If he's sick—and dying—then why in the world would you come looking for me? I'd think you'd be happy to have me long gone."

"Where'd you get that idea?"

David's laugh was more a snort and he shook his head. "What's it been—Danny Boy?" Daniel cringed as he heard his brother use his favorite cruel epithet. "What's it been? Twelve years? You haven't been pounding on doors all these years looking for me, have you?"

"No," admitted Daniel, his head lowered. This would not be easy. David was never diplomatic and he would not cut him any slack. "Most of the last twelve years I've been much too busy running the company and taking care of the family—the family that you deserted, by the way--to play detective."

"So," said David, "what's changed? I know the old man—obviously better than you. He kicked me out of his life—out of his family twelve years ago and told me never to return. I'm just following orders, bro. He's iron—stone. He'll never change. No, Danny Boy, you're here for another reason. I'm not sure what—but it's not at Father's command. Believe me, Father doesn't want me back and he'll never want me back even when he's on death's doorstep."

"Sometimes, David," said Daniel, cautiously attempting to find an approach that might soften his brother's heart, "we have to take the first step. Did you ever consider that maybe if you were to return—apologize—that he might forgive you--that things might be different?"

"You're such a fool," replied David, laughing.

"Maybe," agreed Daniel, "and maybe this was a fool's errand, but David, I had to try. If I don't try to reunite you and Father now—I'll never get another chance."

David shook his head. "You poor schmuck," he guffawed. Standing, he sauntered into the kitchen, opened the refrigerator door and retrieved two beers. He returned and threw one to Daniel and plopped back in the recliner where he opened his and took a long chug.

"Uh, thanks," said Daniel, "I appreciate it. It was a long drive." He sipped the beer from the can. "Good."

"Yeah," said David, "Look, I'm sorry you wasted your time. There was a reason I went incognito and this was part of it." He gestured broadly. "I figured if you knew where I was you'd try to find me. But, believe me, it's a waste. Father doesn't want me back. He would not be grateful if you brought me back and I don't intend to go back. So, here's a beer for your trouble, but your drive was for nothing."

"Not nothing," said Daniel, "Even if you don't return with me—and I haven't given up trying to convince you—it's worth it to me just to see you again—to talk to you—to see you and see what you're doing. You're my brother, for God's sake."

"What you see is what you get," said David, outstretching his arms.

"My investigator tells me you're working on a graduate degree," prompted Daniel.

"Yeah," replied David, "got a Master's in English literature and now I'm working on a doctorate in creative writing. That would really impress the old man, wouldn't it?"

"It's further than I've gone."

"Which is?"

"MBA. Kind of a waste, I suppose. Running Bridgewater Carpets is mostly a hands-on business," he explained, "but you'd know that. You worked there during the summers while you were in high school too."

"Probably the most useless, boring work I've ever done."

"Yes, it comes back to me now. There were certainly lots of battles between you and Father about the direction your life should take."

"And he felt he was the one to decide what that direction should be."

"I know," agreed Daniel, "he can be autocratic, David. I actually live with him."

"Lucky you."

"My investigator tells me you work part-time as a disc jockey."

"Yeah," said David, "very part-time—only four hours on Saturday night—really Sunday morning. That's why I'm sleeping late today, 'cause I have to stay up so late tonight."

"What's your program called?"

"Oh, God, Danny Boy," snickered David, "My 'program' doesn't really have a name. I play alternative rock—you may have heard of 'Goth' or 'emo' music. There's not a huge demand for it in Reardon, but there is a small fan base that supports my four hour show, so I guess you could say I'm sort of a minor celebrity within a certain group."

"Is this the reason for the hair?" Daniel asked, gesturing to David's spiky, puffed up hair style.

"It's romantic," replied David, "like Poe. Tragic. girls like it."

"Ah!" said Daniel, smiling, "You're a rock star!"

"No," said David, sighing, "but I wish. I spend most of my time writing my dissertation that I..... Well, I spend a lot of time writing. How about you? I assume Father has you hop-hop-hopping at the plant?" He took a deep swig from his can and leaned back in the recliner, expecting a lengthy story.

"At first, he did," responded Daniel, "but as time went by and he got older, I pretty much took over the day to day running of things."

"How exciting for you," said David, giving him a mock toast with the beer can.

"I like it," said Daniel, "particularly the people there. It's a family." They each stared at the other and continued drinking. "And truly," he continued finally, "I believe you might like them, if you would consider..."

"No, no, no," David cut him off. "Not going to happen. I'm fine where I am, Danny Boy. You're wasting your breath."

"Maybe," replied Daniel, "but won't you at least give me a chance to try to convince you?"

Daniel looked at him, staring for a long time. "I'm not easy to convince."

"What harm would it do? You visit with your brother for a few hours—days?"

"It's a waste of your time, as I said."

"Let me be the judge of that."

A much longer pause as David twirled his bottle between his palms and stared at the floor. "You could come by the station and be a guest on my show tonight."

"Oh, I couldn't do that," said Daniel, flustered, "I mean I couldn't be a guest—I don't know anything...."

"Hey, just kidding," said David, holding up his palms, "but just drop by and I'll show you around the studio. You can see my domain for a change. I spent more than enough time at that carpet plant than I'd care to think about."

"I guess I could do that." He smiled. David stood and walked over and grabbed the bottle. "I'd offer you some food, but I'm..."

"No, let me treat you," said Daniel.

"I have to finish a paper for class, but.."

"And I need to find a hotel,"

"Hey, look, Danny Boy, you could stay here but, you can see I don't have much space..."

"Don't apologize. I saw a place on my way in. I'll meet you back here for supper, okay? About five? I'll take us somewhere nice, okay?" He stood and headed for the doorway.

"Great," said David, smiling. "That should give me enough time—to get everything done."

Chapter 21

Present time--Wednesday morning, December 19

"I'm sorry," he whispered, his lips touching her ear. She had finally fallen asleep after crying and feeling miserable for most of the night. As she opened her eyes, she realized it was morning, as she could see the sun sparkling through her bedroom window.

"Oh, Rocky," she cried, turning to him and grabbing his neck, "I couldn't sleep at all with you out there in the living room. Don't ever do that again."

"I'm a jerk," he agreed, sitting beside her on the bed. "I couldn't sleep either. Of course, the couch isn't very comfortable. Could be part of it." She punched him playfully in the arm, sniffling.

"I know I should have called you the minute Shoop came into my office and asked me to listen to the tape of the murder," she said, in a rush to explain her behavior of the last day. "Everything just seemed to snowball and pretty soon it had just gotten out of hand."

"How is it out of hand?" he asked, looking worried. "Is someone threatening you?"

"Oh, no," she assured him, and gave him another hug, "Nothing like that. There are quite a few people, actually, working on the tape."

"Oh?"

"Yes," she explained. "Truly, anyone who listened to Ballard's show on Saturday night could—hypothetically—have a recording of the murder. It's not like it's a secret. Lot's of people have heard it."

"So you reason that the more people who know about it, the safer you are," he asked, brows lifted, expecting an answer.

"I wasn't thinking about safety…"

"That's a given, Speed Racer," he said, and then quickly replaced his sullen face with a fake smile.

"I'm thinking more about identifying the killer—as Snoop requested. I reason the more people working on the problem the quicker it will be solved."

"And who—may I ask—is working on it—besides you?"

"Willard, of course," she responded, "I mean, he's an expert on dialect. He determined right away that the killer was probably Southern."

"I thought the killer didn't say anything."

"We think he does—briefly," she said, "and we think from our analysis that it is a he."

"A southern man?" questioned Rocky, shrugging. "That could be anyone."

"I know," she agreed, "so now I also have Mitchell working on it too. He knows a lot about guns so I thought he might be able to figure out something from the gunshot. Also, my graduate acoustics class. I sort of turned it into a class project and they're all working on it too."

"Maybe you should put an ad in the newspaper—calling all detectives. Help Pamela Barnes decipher the mysterious recording and solve a murder."

"I don't think that's necessary…." He was making fun of her to cover his concern.

"I was kidding," he said, shaking his head and leaning back on the headboard. "I hate to tell you, but it's after seven."

"Oh, my God," she replied, "I'll be late if I don't get going."

"I'm going to go make you breakfast," he said to her, protruding his lower lip, "It's my penance for last night."

"Oh, I'll think of a much better penance for you tonight," she smiled at him.

"Good, I deserve punishment," he responded, then looking closely at her in the increasingly lighter room, "Your eyes are all bloodshot. Now, I really feel terrible. I'm going to go make you that breakfast."

"Okay," she said lightly, then touching his arm as he rose to leave, "if you really want to help, Rocky, you could ask around in your department about Ballard. You know, find out if anyone knows anything about him—if he had any enemies. All I know about him is what Trudi told us on Sunday."

"Yes, Inspector," he said, saluting, "But don't push your luck."

She quickly got ready, noticing what Rocky had already seen. Her eyes were horribly red. This was what happened when she was awake half the night and spent most of it crying. But it couldn't be helped. She had to get to work. She tried to cover her eyes with extra eye shadow and more foundation under her lower lids, but nothing seemed to help. Her students would just have to see what she looked like after an "all-nighter" as they would say. As she stared at her reflection, she realized that it wasn't half-bad—except of course for the red eyes. She had a head of shiny, shoulder length natural blond hair, clear skin, virtually perfect teeth, and her figure was ample. Nothing would get her to say "fat." She envisioned herself as one of those nudes in a Botticelli painting, lying around in a group eating grapes, their folds of cellulite exposed with pride. She dressed quickly in a stylish skirt and sweater outfit and put in a pair of her favorite earrings. After a brief but enjoyable breakfast with her delightfully contrite husband, she was on her way.

As she entered the main office, otherwise known these days as Christmas Central, to greet Jane Marie (and check on any new gossip) and pick up her mail, she discovered that Mitchell Marks had just arrived himself and was asking her to stop in his office for a moment. As she still had a half hour before her first class, she entered the "trophy" room as she often thought of Mitchell's office and took up a seat before his large desk. Mitchell scurried around to his side of the desk and sat.

"I'm glad I caught you, Pamela," he said. "I've been listening to the recording and I think I may have a possibility for you."

"Oh?" she said. "Wonderful. What?"

"Here again," he explained, his blue eyes focused intently on hers, "My God, Pamela, what happened to your eyes? Did you have an allergic reaction to something?"

"No," she said, thinking that her efforts at cover-up had been for naught, "just difficulty sleeping last night."

"Oh," he said, then continued with his original thought, "Anyway, I'm thinking there is something strange about the gunshot on the recording."

"How so?"

"I tried to picture how this murder occurred, you see. Listening to the recording, the killer appears to enter a door. The victim is at the microphone. The killer shoots the victim from a certain distance—I'm not certain what…"

"About ten feet," she interjected. "I took measurements in the studio the other day."

"Good," he continued, "But, as I said, I'm a gun collector and hunter—not a ballistics expert, but the sound of the gunshot—oh, I know it's a hand gun—not a rifle, but even so, there's something strange about it. I can't quite put my finger on it but you might want to listen to it yourself. You are the acoustics expert."

"But not a ballistics expert," she noted, sighing.

"Even so," he said, with excitement, "there is definitely something strange about the gun shot. Take it from someone who shoots a lot of guns. That's about all I can tell you, but I'm going to continue listening to it and see if I can't come up with something more specific."

"Good," replied Pamela, nodding. "Thanks, Mitchell, for your efforts. Wouldn't it be amazing if our department could solve this case?"

"We'd have to give up teaching psychology," he said, with a laugh, "and go into forensics." With that, she rose and left Mitchell Marks to his work. She passed Jane Marie coming in with a stack of papers as she was leaving.

"So, Dr. Barnes," said Jane Marie, softly, to the accompaniment of "The Little Drummer Boy," "did you break the case yet?"

"Not yet," Pamela replied to the young secretary, "but I'm working on it." She left the office, this time avoiding the temptation of all of Jane Marie's Christmas sweets, almost skipping. She had a new clue—or at least a new line of questioning. Rocky had promised he would look into Ballard over at the English Department, and she had two colleagues and an entire class also working on the mystery tape. Boy, did she know how to delegate.

Pamela hurried up to her office and made it to her morning classes with time to spare. After lecturing for several hours and enjoying an especially nice lunch that Rocky had packed (he obviously was feeling tremendously guilty because not only had breakfast been fantastic, lunch was the best ever), she leaned back on her couch, slipped out of her heels which were just a pinch too tight about this time every day, and put her stocking covered feet up on the sofa to sip her licorice tea.

She wondered if she would see Joan and Arliss today, but if they didn't show, she'd see them tonight, because they had planned one of their girl outings to check out the Blue Poppy in downtown Reardon. Maybe there, she would actually find someone who knew Ted Ballard—or who knew about him. Up until now, the murder victim remained a mystery. Okay, she said to herself, enough loafing. Get busy, girl. She slipped her shoes back on and wandered over to her desk, thermos of tea in hand. She sat down in her rolling chair and powered up her sound analysis program—loading the CD recording of Ted Ballard's murder into her hard drive.

Almost instantly, the spectrographic output of the disc jockey's final words appeared on the screen. She set the cursor to the left hand side where the sound began and hit the *play* button. The short segment that ended in the gunshot emitted from her desktop speakers. Focusing in on Mitchell's suspicion that there was "something strange" about the gunshot, she highlighted the gunshot and a second or two before and after it, and played it over and over a number of times, listening for anything that might seem out of place. Unfortunately, knowing nothing about guns and ballistics, this procedure eventually proved a waste of her time. She returned to the beginning of the short recording and played it many times so that she could focus on the brief vocalization that she believed was the voice of the killer. She wanted to see how the killer's only produced sound fit in with what Ballard was saying. She played the recording and closed her eyes. She tried to envision the little station that she had just visited the other day. She remembered sitting in the disc jockey's chair—where Ballard was sitting when he was killed. She envisioned the glass door that the killer must have entered when he came into the small radio station. She envisioned these two men (she felt in her heart that they were both men) as they stood there. She pictured them as she played the tape. She tried to envision what Ballard was doing when he was talking—what the killer was doing at the same time. She realized the exact point in the recording when the killer must have revealed the gun. It was almost the same time as when the killer made the vocal sound—something like a gasp, but more of a vowel sound. It was almost at the same time as when Ballard said "What the?" He must have thought that the killer was kidding when he brought out the gun.

She wondered as her class had wondered the other night why Ballard never indicated anything that would identify his killer. He managed to say quite a bit between the time the killer entered and he was shot. She thought, that's probably more to do with him being a disc jockey—he's probably used to spewing out his thoughts on air. He was just giving a running account of what was happening. He didn't identify the killer, she reasoned, because he didn't know the killer. Or did he? Was there anything in this recording to indicate that Ballard had any idea who the killer was?

She also wondered about the way the recording ended. Her class had noted that. Had someone turned off the microphone? She remembered the microphone on the disc jockey's desk. It had a very noticeable on/off switch. Did someone turn it off? If so, it couldn't have been Ballard—he was dead. Unless, she thought, unless he accidentally bumped the on/off switch as he slumped to the floor—like Charlotte Clark did when she was struggling against her killer in the computer lab last year. Maybe the recording just sounded like it was turned off and wasn't really turned off until the police and the station manager, Mr. Gallagher, arrived at least a half hour later. She didn't know. If the killer turned off the microphone, she wondered, why? Why would the killer do that? Why wouldn't the killer just leave?

She repeated the tape again—and then again. She went back again to the gunshot. Mitchell thought it was strange, but it didn't seem strange to her—it just seemed loud. Maybe she should learn something about ballistics. No time like the present, she thought. Luckily, no students seemed to be visiting her today during office hours. That was typical. Some days it was busy, and some days, like today, it was a tomb. She Googled "ballistics" and "hand guns" and various other terms in an effort to understand the acoustics of gunshots. My goodness, she thought, there was so much to it. Much different than the acoustics of human voices.

Her phone ringing drew her from her intense concentration. It was Shoop.

"Dr. Barnes," he greeted her. "How are you coming on that analysis?"

"Detective," she replied, "Am I your only lead? You called my house last night and told my husband about this."

"My, oh my," replied Shoop, "Did I cause trouble in paradise?" He laughed.

"No," she said, bristling, "you did not. But, I would prefer to inform my husband myself about my crime-fighting activities. I'd rather he not hear about them from you."

"Fair enough," answered Shoop, "Anyway, the reason I called was that I've received the updated autopsy report on Ballard and although it's fairly standard and contains nothing much that would affect your part in this investigation, there is one unusual item that I'm thinking might be of interest to you."

"And that would be?"

"The entry angle of the bullet," he replied. "You seemed so concerned at the radio station about measuring distances—from the microphone to the door and so forth, that I thought you might like to know that the coroner found that the bullet that killed Ballard entered from below. That is, the bullet entered near Ballard's nose and lodged in his brain. This would suggest that the killer was sitting, kneeling, or was very short and or that Ballard was standing."

"Thank you, Detective," she replied, "I don't know what to make of this information. Do you?"

"Nope," said the Detective, "I don't have a clue. The killer couldn't have been sitting as there were no chairs by the door and I see no reason for him to kneel. From the recording, it doesn't sound like Ballard stands up—does it?"

"No," she agreed, "there would be a noticeable change in the volume level if he did."

"So, I guess it means our killer was a midget."

"Oh, Detective, do you know if the police officers or the station manager turned off the microphone when they arrived?"

"No," replied Shoop, checking his notes, "It was already turned off. Gallagher checked that immediately. He didn't want his discussions with the police going out over the air waves. "

They chatted pleasantly for a few more minutes and then hung up. Pamela, thinking about the new information, returned to the online ballistics information sites. What in the world? Why would the bullet come in from such a low angle? There was no reason for it. None that she could see. She started to read the ballistics sites more carefully—particularly the explanation of how gunshots were displayed acoustically. Now here was something that looked relatively familiar. When a gunshot was recorded and displayed on a spectrograph, a fairly traditional profile was created. Ballistics experts could determine a huge array of information about a gun or a bullet merely by examining the acoustic display of a certain gunshot. One thing they could determine, she learned, was distance. The gunshot created an acoustically unique profile that indicated in great detail the exact distance of the gun to the target as compared to the recording device. She studied the material, reading over and over, the explanation of how the distance was determined from the gun to the target. Primarily, she realized that the initial explosion from the gun created the longest (or tallest) output on the acoustic display. This very noticeable spike was a fair indication of the location of the gun to the recording device or microphone. The closer the gun to the microphone, the closer the spike to the beginning of the acoustic output. In Ballard's case, the distance was short— only ten feet, but Ballard was sitting immediately in front of the mic and the killer was much further away. The display should have begun, then there should have been a brief momentary delay and then the spike should have occurred on the display about the same time as the bullet hit Ballard and the CD should have recorded the bullet hitting Ballard—after all, Ballard and the mic were in virtually the same position. This is not what happened. On her visual display, as she listened to the recording, the spike from the initial explosion of the gun, occurred immediately—as if the person shooting the gun was holding it directly in front of the microphone. She listened for a sound after that to indicate the bullet had hit Ballard. It should be loud. She could hear no such sound. What did that mean?

Chapter 22

Previous week--December 15, Saturday afternoon

When Daniel returned to David's apartment at five o'clock—exactly at five o'clock as he had promised—he was excited. The first meeting with his brother had gone better than he had expected. Yes, David was belligerent but he'd expected that. At least, he was willing to talk to him and that gave Daniel hope. After he'd left David's apartment earlier in the day, he'd been busy. He'd found a nice, nearby hotel and checked in, grabbed a quick sandwich in the hotel's small restaurant, and then gone to his room to rest and call Harold Vickers to check on his father's condition and to report on his progress. Vickers had informed him that his father was holding his own—no change—for good or bad. That was all Daniel felt he could hope for at least for now. Vickers was delighted to hear from Daniel that he'd found David in good shape and at least willing to talk. He wished him luck at dinner and then Daniel had taken a quick nap. He didn't want to call Amy in the middle of the day when he knew she was at work and would not appreciate being disturbed. They were trying to keep their relationship secret and so far, had done a good job of that.

Now he stood at his brother's rickety screen door again and knocked for the second time. This time, David opened it immediately. Smiling, he led Daniel inside.

"Hey," said Daniel, noticing a change, "you shaved. Hope that isn't for me."

"Nah," replied David, "I was getting kind of scraggly. Maybe you inspired me to clean up my act."

"Glad I could be of service," replied Daniel. As his eyes adjusted to the darkened apartment, he noticed that David had straightened up the place and had set out beers and several boxes of obviously fresh pizza."

"Just trying to be a good host," said David, anticipating his comment. "I thought we might just eat here. More comfortable, don't ya think? Plus, I've still got lots of school stuff to do before my show tonight."

"Oh," said Daniel, somewhat deflated, "I was hoping we could spend the evening together. You know, talk about old times."

"Talk away, Danny Boy," responded his brother, arm outstretched towards the food on the counter, "and make yourself at home. I'm sure you'll be thoroughly bored with me before long." Daniel smiled and shook his head. Then with a shrug he peeked into one of the pizza boxes, helping himself to a few slices of pepperoni and a beer.

"Don't you have a table?"

"Nah," said David. "Just sit wherever you want in the living room." Daniel placed his beer on one of the end tables and carefully sat on the end of the sofa—which was without its blanket today—that remained folded at the other end. David was rifling through the pizza and piling several pieces on a plate. Grabbing a beer, he headed for the recliner. They were now in the same positions they had maintained during their initial talk this morning.

"You know," said Daniel, "I would have been happy to take you out somewhere nice."

"Hey, I'm the host—not you. This is 'nice' enough for me. My home—my food." He scowled—then suddenly smiled brightly. Daniel slowly took a bite of his pizza. "Besides, this is the best pizza ever. Try it. Go on! It's great." Daniel took another bite. "Right?" Daniel nodded obligingly.

"So," began Daniel, slowly, attempting he hoped to begin a discussion that would eventually lead to a successful plea for David's return. "How did you—uh—find yourself here? In this town? Uh...working on a graduate degree?"

"Oh, the life history! The sob story!" David had finished his few slices of pizza and had returned to the counter for second helpings. He remained standing, munching on a new slice as he narrated his tale. "Wayward son refuses to follow in father's footsteps. Father kicks wayward son out of family and tells him never to return. Wayward son leaves in disgrace never to be heard from again. There you have it—from your end anyway. From my end, it was actually a blessing. The old man was a monster—determined to run my life for me and—strange as it may seem—I preferred to live my own life. So—I left—quite willingly. Yes, it was hard at first. Odd jobs, and as you know—I changed my identity, although as it turned out that was probably unnecessary because the old man never really made any attempts to find me—until now—and I guess that was probably more your doing than his. And of course—you can see how changing my identity helped in keeping me safe when someone was truly determined---to find me." With these last three words he turned to Daniel and looked at him directly with what Daniel thought was anger—maybe annoyance. Then suddenly, he smiled and started eating the pizza slice he had been using as a baton.

"And you're in graduate school?" asked Daniel, cautiously.

"That I am, Danny Boy," responded David. "Got a BA in Dramatic Arts, then came here and whizzed through a Master's degree in English. About four years ago, I started working on a doctoral degree here in English—creative writing, actually. I've finished my course work. Only have to complete my dissertation and I'll be done. It's almost complete—just a few finishing touches needed—that's what I'm trying to get done—got a really demanding dissertation advisor. Plus, I'm a graduate teaching assistant so I teach four sections of freshman composition."

"My God," said Daniel, "I'm impressed. I always did terrible in composition."

"So, you wouldn't be willing to help me grade a stack of student essays that has to be finished by Monday?"

"Sorry," said Daniel, laughing, "You're on your own there."

"Yeah," said David, "guess you picked a bad weekend to visit. If I didn't have so much work to get done by Monday, I'd be able to drive you around and show you the sights of Reardon."

"David, I didn't come here for sight-seeing. I came here to try to get you to return."

"I know, because the old man is sick and about to die," David said, in a mocking sing-song voice.

"Would it kill you? Couldn't you come back for just a day or two? I mean, maybe after you finish these grading and writing obligations you have for Monday?"

"'Fraid not, Danny Boy," said David, with a shrug. "Besides, I know you don't believe this, but the old man has no interest in seeing me. In fact, I'd venture a guess that if he did, it would probably kill him on the spot."

"I don't believe that. You're his son. No matter what caused the rift—he surely would be overjoyed to have you return."

"Don't bet on it."

"Will you at least think about it?" His iPhone buzzed unexpectedly and Daniel reached in his pocket and answered it. "Hello. Harold? Yes? Oh, no! Yes, I am. In fact, I'm here right now. I'm trying to talk him into it. What did Knowles say? I see. Okay. Keep me posted."

"Bad news?"

"Father just had another one of his seizures. He had one last week too. The doctor doesn't think it's a good sign."

"A seizure?"

"Right—on top of congestive heart failure. David, he doesn't have long. Really, just a brief visit could mean so much. It wouldn't cure him—I'm not suggesting that. It would just bring him some needed closure. He's holding such animosity in his heart because of this feud between the two of you. If you could be the one to break the impasse, I think it would relieve his mind tremendously."

"You think?"

"I do."

"I have to think about it. Who was that on the phone?"

"Harold Vickers. He's our company—and family attorney. Almost like an uncle, really. Don't you remember him? I guess not. Anyway, he's been a rock through all of this. He was the one who found the investigator who tracked you down."

"And who is Knowles?"

"Oh, he's father's personal physician."

"I bet you're checking in with them daily. It probably killed you to have to leave the old man's side for a whole day, didn't it?"

"Yes, actually. I check in as often as I can. Sometimes I just call Bernice."

"Bernice? You mean that grouchy woman who was the old man's secretary?"

"Still there. But she's hardly grouchy." Daniel had finished his pizza and beer and had risen and walked toward the kitchen in search of a napkin.

"What'd you need?"

"A napkin?"

"And you can't use your shirt sleeve?"

"What?"

"Never mind, Danny Boy. We live in two different worlds, don't we?" He zipped around the kitchen counter and scrounged under the sink where he finally pulled out a roll of paper towels—partially used. "Here, Mr. Clean."

"Thanks."

"Yeah." He stood beside his brother, closely scrutinizing him from top to bottom. "Still the clean-cut yuppie I remember. Button-down collar, chinos, nice loafers."

"I suppose so. You've changed quite a bit," said Daniel, trying to assert himself against his brother's denigration of his appearance. "What's with the hair and all the dark clothing?"

"It's my image. I'm Black Vulture."

"Who?"

"My radio name—Black Vulture. The hero of the local alternative music fans. I told you I'm a minor celebrity around here."

"And this Black Vulture dresses like a vampire?"
"It's even better when I go out."
"I'd like to see that."
"Oh, you can. Well, I shouldn't say when I go out—but when I'm in my character—like tonight on my show."
"Your radio show?"
"Yeah. I get all fixed up and it puts me in the mood."
"I would like to see that."
"Then, why don't you stop by the station tonight? You can see me in my element. Full Black Vulture mode. I'd say just stick around and follow me over but I've really got to get those essays done before my show."
"It wouldn't bother you to have me watch you."
"Nah," replied David. "As long as you're quiet."
"I can do that. Where is this radio station?"
"Where are you staying?"
"It's on the highway I came in on, further out east—Rambler's Rest Stop."
"Rambler's. Sure. I know it. Actually you're not too far from the station at all. Here, let me draw you a map." He found a small writing pad and a pencil on the counter and drew a quick sketch for Daniel of how to get to radio station KRDN. "Now, look, I don't really get going until after midnight—so don't show up until after that, okay?"
"Sure. I'm exhausted actually. I think I'll go take a nap until later and then I'll find my way over there. It'll be fun to see what you do as—Black Vulture!"
"It'll be fun, all right!" repeated David.

Chapter 23

Present time, December 19, Wednesday, late afternoon

It was hard to believe it was still only about four o'clock in the afternoon. As they entered the out of the way dive on a side street in downtown Reardon, the place was virtually pitch black. As the outside door whooshed close from the wind, Pamela, Joan, and Arliss stood shivering together, as they attempted to warm up and let their eyes adjust to the darkened interior. The Blue Poppy might as well have been named the Dark Poppy. Did they have any lighting at all? wondered Pamela. While she was pondering this question, a somber voice asked, "You ladies want a table?" Pamela turned to her left where she saw a young woman wearing a white (a delightfully visible white) apron.

"Yes," she responded, turning to peer at Joan and Arliss who both looked as mystified as she felt. The young woman motioned to them and they followed her through the darkness around several walls until they were eventually in a cavernous setting full of wooden tables at one end, a long wooden bar on one side and a small platform at the far end. Now she could actually see because ambient light from spotlights aimed at the platform allowed her to view the interior of the Blue Poppy. She had a strong déjà vu experience of a hippie poetry reading marathon. The young woman motioned to them to an empty table (most of the tables were empty—it was, after all, only four o'clock—not the time when most creatures of the night were out prowling).

The three women removed their outer coats and placed them over their chairs before they seated themselves at the small table. The table was so small, in fact, that all of their knees were smashed together. One chair remained empty, its back to the stage. Pamela hoped they would see or hear some performance because she wanted to get a sense of what Black Vulture—Ted Ballard—was actually like and this was evidently the place to find that out.

The young hostess handed the three women a long handbill which turned out to be a type of menu. She hurried away promising to return shortly for their order.

"This is weird," said Arliss.

"Yes, dear," agreed Joan, patting her hand, as she typically did when she sensed that Arliss might be headed for a meltdown, "but fun weird. Let's just drink it all in." Joan closed her eyes and gestured as if she were pushing nearby aromas closer to her nostrils.

"This looks actually good," said Pamela, reading the long, curly menu. "A Tulip Kiss. It has Amaretto, chocolate, and vanilla ice cream."

"Really?" said Joan, perking up. "Let me see." She unrolled her paper menu and began perusing the various alcoholic offerings. "Ooo. Yummy."

"Pam," said Arliss, "do you really think you're going to learn something meaningful about this Vulture fellow from this place?"

"I hope so," replied Pamela, "Maybe we'll hear a performance. That would really help. Don't you think?"

"Vulcan's Coffin!" exclaimed Arliss, reading from her rolled up menu, "Can you imagine? It sounds disgusting!"

"Have you ladies decided what you'd like?" asked the non-smiling waitress who had appeared miraculously at their table.

"I definitely want one of these Tulip Kisses," said Pamela.

"Oh," said Joan, "and I'll have a Bloody Lover's Revenge." She smiled coyly.

"Arliss?" asked Pamela looking over at her friend, her head buried in the list of hundreds of strange drink names. "Arliss?" Arliss remained unresponsive. "She'll have a "Vulcan's Coffin."

"No!" said Arliss.

"Yes," said Pamela, taking the menu from Arliss's hands, rolling it up, and handing it back to the waitress.

"A number four, a 21, and a 33," said the bland woman, writing the order on her pad without comment, and then disappearing again into the darkness.

"Now why did you do that, Pam?" pouted Arliss.

"Because otherwise you would sit here until closing time trying to make up your mind. If you don't like Vulcan's Coffin, just order something else. As long as it has alcohol in it—it should work."

"Yes, my dear," agreed Joan. "You need to unwind. You're far too uptight about all this wedding business. Just sit back and let Bob's mother handle things. That's what I'd do."

"I'm not you, Joan," countered Arliss, crossing her arms—in lieu of crossing her legs which were frozen solidly against Pamela's and Joan's kneecaps under the small table. "Oh, look, I think they're going to play music." She pointed towards the stage and appeared to be right. Several people (they could have been men or women) dressed all in black appeared on the small platform and began setting up equipment, and turning on amplifiers. One of them set up a microphone center stage and placed a wooden stool behind it.

"Not too many people here for a performance," Pamela said, looking around. "We must be the largest part of their audience. Do you see anyone else?"

"I think I see some people in the back," said Joan, peering over Pamela's shoulder. "It's hard to tell in this darkness."

The glum waitress that had taken their order returned with a tray of their drinks. She slowly placed each beverage in front of each woman.

"These look amazing!" exclaimed Pamela.

"If they put Gummy Bears in this I'm going to puke," said Arliss.

"It's what you wanted, " replied Joan.

"No, I didn't," said Arliss, "It's what Pamela made me order."

A tall blonde woman entered the stage and stood beside the microphone. Clapping from a few unseen people ensued. Pamela immediately joined in enthusiastically and Joan and Arliss followed suit. The blonde woman bowed and took her place on the stool and adjusted the mic. She opened what appeared to be a small notebook and began reading what sounded to be poetry—although Pamela wasn't certain. Pamela recognized much of the imagery that she had seen in the poetry that Trudi Muldoon had showed them in Theodore Ballard's dissertation. There was lots of death, gloom, darkness, torture, unrequited love, and other horrific images. The blonde reader spoke in a low, rumbling voice into the microphone:

> "Death is daring me
> Death is calling me
> Come to me, Death.
> Come be my lover.
> Make love to me, Death.
> Hold me in your arms
> And smother me
> With eternal kisses"

"Gross," said Arliss, cringing.

"Now, dear," said Joan, "doesn't a Vulcan's Coffin sound like a nice idea?"

The woman continued reading as activity went on around her. The bar tender continued making drinks—even using his blender on high speed which was very loud. The young reader didn't seem to be cognizant of or bothered by the noise.

The sour waitress arrived back at their table just as Pamela had finished slurping through her Tulip Kiss. Wanting to drink another, but realizing that she had driven to their present location in her Civic and not wanting to end up in jail (that would really set off both Rocky and Detective Shoop), she pulled the waitress's sleeve and whispered in her ear, "Do you always have entertainment in the afternoon?

The waitress responded in a monotone, her lips barely moving, "We usually have readers late in the afternoon most days. There are lots of would-be poets who want to perform. In the evenings we have bands. If you want to hear some of the bands, you'll have to stick around until eight or so."

"Did you happen to know this Black Vulture fellow who was killed on Saturday night at KRDN?"

The waitress looked at her for a second, as if to sense the sincerity of her question. Then she intoned, "We all knew him. Not well, really. But he was here often. He introduced a lot of bands that play here on his show."

"Did anyone know him well?"

"I don't think so. Black Vulture was really a loner. Too bad, too. There were a lot of girls in his classes—at the University, you know, who had a crush on him. But, he never seemed interested in anyone that I could tell. Mostly just interested in the music."

"Alternative music?"

"Yeah," she replied, shrugged and then turned abruptly and headed back to the kitchen.

"Pamela!" Pamela looked around to see who was calling her name. A tall, gawky form in a long navy blue raincoat was headed their way, squeezing between tables. When she arrived and stood before the three women, backlit by the spotlights from the platform, Pamela realized that she was looking at Trudi Muldoon, Rocky's colleague from the English Department.

"Trudi," she exclaimed, "What brings you here?"

"I'm here to find out more about Ted," said Trudi.

"Really?" asked Pamela. "That's why we're here. Trudi, my friends and colleagues Joan Bentley and Arliss MacGregor from the Psychology Department. This is Trudi Muldoon, from the English Department. Her office is right across from Rocky's—and she was Ted Ballard's dissertation advisor."

"Do tell," said Joan, brightly.

"Could I interest you in a Vulcan's Coffin?" asked Arliss, extending her half-finished drink to Trudi.

Trudi's auspicious appearance enlivened the conversation as the three women had an unending series of questions for her. Pamela repeated for Trudi the waitress's response about

Ted Ballard not having any close friends but that a lot of the female students had a crush on him.

"That doesn't surprise me," said Trudi, who had opted for a Tulip Kiss too. Arliss continued to prod on the crunchy morsels in her drink. "He adopted that Romantic—and by romantic, I mean with a capital "R" look. The longish hair, dark, brooding look, dark clothes, boots, and even sometimes make-up."

"Like lipstick?" asked Arliss, sticking out her tongue in disgust.

"No," replied Trudi, "typically eye liner. I thought maybe he used white make-up sometimes. He was less obvious about it on campus. I got the idea that he pushed the envelope more when he was out and about in his persona as this 'Black Vulture.'"

"Is that why you came here, Trudi?" asked Joan.

"Yes," replied Trudi, slurping the last of her Tulip Kiss. "This is really good. But, yes, my students had told me that he tended to hang out here and had a following. He also recruited alternative bands from bands that played here, so I thought I might learn something if I came and waited around a while."

"You didn't happen to mention your plans to Rocky, did you?" asked Pamela, carefully.

"No," Trudi answered, "should I have?"

"Tell me, Trudi," said Pamela, obviously feeling a bit emboldened by the amazing Tulip Kiss, leaning against the table and staring at Trudi, "does your husband approve of your investigating the death of your student?"

"What?" said Trudi, sputtering.

"My dear," said Joan to Trudi, interjecting her body between the two women, "Pamela's husband is very protective and doesn't like her to get involved in police matters, which, as you know, she has definitely done."

"Oh, I see," replied Trudi, laughing, her large front teeth protruding, "truthfully, I think it's wonderful that Rocky cares so much about your welfare, Pamela. My husband is so totally wrapped up making model airplanes in the garage, that I hardly think he knows when I leave and when I return." She laughed sadly, but loudly.

"We all have our crosses to bear," exclaimed Arliss, pushing back a lock of her flyaway black hair and pulling on a chunk of Vulcan's Coffin that was stuck between her front teeth.

"Don't we though," said Joan, smiling as she glanced around the table at her three companions. "So many problems caused by love." The three women looked at her as she nodded wisely and sipped her drink which was only barely touched.

Chapter 24

Previous week--December 15, Saturday evening

After a pleasant supper in the restaurant of the Rambler's Rest Stop, Daniel had returned to his room where he relaxed and napped for a while. Around eight o'clock he pressed Amy's number on his iPhone and she answered on the second ring. She sounded sleepy.

"Don't tell me you're in bed this early?" he asked, leaning back against the headboard of his bed.

"Oh, Dan," she responded, "I must have caught a virus or something. I felt terrible this morning and I didn't even think I'd make it in to work."

"I hope you stayed in bed," he replied, immediately concerned, more by the sound of her voice than her report.

"No, actually," she said, "I'm better now. It must have been one of the 24 hour bugs. I'm just beat though. Sam's was packed. Have you met David?"

"Yes," he said, "actually, we're getting together again later tonight."

"Really?"

"Yeah," he replied. "You know he's a disc jockey. He's got a Saturday night show that's evidently a cult favorite around here. I'm going to go by the radio studio later and watch him do his thing."

"That sounds promising," she said, "and does he seem to be willing to return with you to see your father?"

"That part—not so much," he replied, sighing, "but I haven't given up. I think it's more that he's really busy with his graduate program and teaching, plus he doesn't seem to think that father would appreciate him showing up. I tried to convince him otherwise."

"Keep at it," she advised. "If anyone can convince him, it'll be you. You are relentless when you want something."

"I thought I'd never convince you to give me a chance," he whispered softly.

"As I said, relentless," she whispered back.

"Umm, I miss you," he said, "There's just way too much distance between us. Holding my iPhone is not the same as your soft, smooth skin."

"At least we can talk," she said, "besides, I still look a little green, so you might not want to be close to me. I'm probably contagious."

"If you still feel bad tomorrow," he ordered her, "I want you to go to the clinic and get checked out. Better yet, I'll call Knowles tonight and have him stop by your place tomorrow."

"Now how would that look?" she asked. "Dr. Knowles doesn't know about us—unless of course Harold Vickers clued him in. Besides, he has his hands full taking care of your father."

"You're right," Daniel agreed. "But, I don't want you getting worse. If you're not better tomorrow, promise me, you'll go get checked out."

"Yes, Danny," she said, laughing. "My goodness, you sound like my mother used to sound when I came down with a cold or something."

"Your mother isn't around any more," observed Daniel, "so it's a very good thing you have me to take care of you."

"And me to take care of you," she said, pointedly. "I'm still not crazy about you running off to track down your long-lost brother all on your own. You should have some assistance at least, some...."

"Back-up?" He folded his hands behind his head and leaned against the headboard.

"Yes," she agree, "like that Jax fellow. Why didn't he do the chasing down anyway?"

"I told you," he said, "Amy, this is something I have to do myself. David is my brother. This is a personal matter—very personal. I'm the only one who has any hope of convincing David to return. If I can't do it, no one can."

"So," she said, resigned to his determined sound, "you're going to the radio station tonight?"

"Yes," he said, "Station KRDN in Reardon. I've got directions and I'm supposed to meet him over there after midnight. It might be fun. I gotta tell you, seeing him was strange. He looks—well—different. His radio name is...get this...Black Vulture. He says it's his radio name. He dresses all in black...like some movie hero from the silent picture days."

"And he goes to class like that?"

"Not sure," he said. "He was busy grading lots of student essays and trying to finish up something for his dissertation, otherwise I'd probably be there now. We had supper together—or rather—he served me pizza in his apartment."

"He at least sounds conscientious," she noted.

"Definitely one's image of a starving grad student."

"You didn't get the impression that he was at all...bitter...that his father had disowned him?"

"I don't know if he even knows that he is disowned legally. Certainly, he knows that he's disowned emotionally—and doesn't seem to care at all. I know he shows no interest in the carpet business and never has. If he's harboring any resentment or envy—or anything like that—I didn't get the impression."

"If he is resentful, he must know that this would be an ideal opportunity to mend fences with your father."

"Correct," said Daniel, "Father is in a weakened, vulnerable position and if I can David to return and can get the two of them together, Amy, I'm just sure I can bring about a reconciliation."

"You are such an optimist," she exclaimed. "It's one of the main reasons I love you."

"Oh," he sighed, "I thought you loved me for my hard as rock abs and my movie star chiseled features."

"Too funny," she giggled. "I much prefer your slightly pudgy tummy and your sweet little round face."

"You're obviously the only one who does," he pouted.

"I'd better be!"

"I'm swearing on the Bible that I found here in the nightstand next to the bed in my hotel room," he said with conviction. "Can't you see my raised hand?"

She laughed and then added, "Don't make me laugh; it hurts my stomach."

"Sorry, Sweet," he whispered, "I wish I were there with you to gently rub your belly."

"I'm imagining you doing that now," she whispered in a gentle, dreamy voice.

"Just close your eyes and feel the gentle strokes of my hand." Daniel placed the pillow from the bed on his lap and caressed it in soft circles. He closed his eyes as he had ordered Amy to do and the two remained silent, except for the sound of their paired breathing.

"I'm going to fall asleep, Danny," she said eventually.

"Which is a good idea," he said, "it's what you need. I'll let you go, but I'll call you in the morning, okay?"

"Absolutely," she agreed. "Enjoy your trip to the radio station and good luck with your brother."

"Thanks," he replied, "I hope you're feeling better soon. Sleep tight. I'll call you first thing tomorrow. Love you."

"Love you too." They clicked their phones off at the same time. Daniel set the pillow aside and stared at the far wall of the little hotel room. He hoped Amy didn't have anything serious. Maybe he should call Knowles and have him drop by her apartment just in case. No, he reasoned. That would just upset Amy. She probably needed sleep more than anything. If she seemed worse tomorrow when he called, then he'd definitely call Knowles. He was not going to take any chances with her welfare. God, now he felt awful that he was hundreds of miles away and couldn't be there for her. Well, there was nothing he could do about it now. It was after eleven o'clock. He'd better think about getting ready for his foray into the world of alternative music at radio station KRDN.

Chapter 25

Present time--December 20, Thursday

The two Tulip Kisses she had consumed last night at the Blue Poppy were evidently much stronger than she had thought—or than she was used to. Now as she struggled to make it through her morning classes, Pamela wondered if her students could tell that she was—dare she say it?---hungover—and on a Thursday, no less. Even so, the beverage was divine and she'd have another one someday if she ever ventured down to the Blue Poppy. Too bad, she thought, that she had sacrificed her sobriety to try to find some clues about the elusive Ted Ballard, but had come up virtually empty handed.

It was funny that Trudi Muldoon also seemed to be conducting her own research on her recently demised advisee. She and Trudi had bonded last night in their mutual desire to solve the murder. Trudi had supplied her with more personal information about Ballard and she had shared her own discoveries about the audio recording with the English professor. They had agreed to continue to work together until the young man's mysterious death was solved. At least, she thought that's what they had agreed. Trudi had also consumed a few of the Blue Poppy's elegant looking alcoholic drinks and for all Pamela knew, they might have performed one of those blood brother rituals on the small stage in front of her colleagues. Oh my God, she used to be able to hold her liquor better.

Somehow, her classes had ended and she found herself sitting at her desk finishing off the tail end of her sandwich. Today's offering from Rocky was left-over egg salad on a white roll with plain tea. He hated her she was sure. He seemed rather upset over last night's imbibing, but then again, she might not have been reading him right. She was in a bit of a fog when she returned home. She was lucky she had made it home, if truth be told. He was probably worried about her driving "under the influence" as he would say.

Her monitor was on and the ubiquitous gun shot profile was visible. She gave the cursor a press and the sound of Ballard's final words filled her office.

"Oh, Theodore Ballard," she said to the monitor, "who shot you?"

"Still no idea?" said Willard Swinton, as his round head appeared in her door frame.

"Willard," she sighed. "I've listened to this recording at least a hundred times. There's a lot of strange things about it but I'll be damned if I can figure out what they all mean."

"I've been listening too, Pamela," said Willard, entering her office, holding a plastic CD package in his hand, obviously the recording she had made for him of the murder. Willard looked chipper and well rested, his Navy blue pinstriped suit and light blue shirt providing a nice contrast to his chocolate face. "I may have some additional information for you about our mystery speaker."

"You mean the killer."

"All I know is a person speaks at the same time as this Ballard fellow. We have a definite vowel sound that overlaps Ballard's speech. We've already determined that this second speaker is probably male, and probably Southern. I can also add that the person is probably well educated—I mean from a private school."

"Really?"

"Fairly sure," Willard said, smiling and nodding, his print silk bow tie, wobbling up and down over his larynx. "But..."

"Yes?"

"That is not the most important finding I have for you."

"Really?"

"Yes," he came closer to her desk, pointing directly at the CD in its case, "Pamela, as I listened to this recording over and over, particularly the second acoustic line that we believe is the killer and the voice of Ballard himself, I noticed something strange."

"What?" She was beginning to feel like Barbara Walters, question following question.

"I ran an acoustic profile for the fundamental frequency for both voices as well as several other comparisons between the two voices. Of course, I don't have much to go on with the second voice, but there's quite a bit of data for Ballard's voice so...."

"Willard," she interrupted, "what did you find?"

"Both voices are almost identical."

"What?"

"The killer could be Ballard's clone—vocally speaking, that is."

"That doesn't make any sense."

"I know, it doesn't, but truly that's what I found. I can show you the acoustic profiles I ran if you'd like me to demonstrate...."

"No, no," she said, holding up her hands in protest. "I believe you Willard. I just don't get it. How likely is it for two voices to be identical?"

"Not identical," he clarified, "but quite similar. Amazingly similar."

"So our killer sounds like Ted Ballard," she said, thinking aloud.

"Yes," said Willard Swinton, nodding. They both stood silently staring at each other. There were many logical reasons why one voice might sound like another. But it was still very strange. The ringing of Pamela's desk phone startled them both. Pamela answered it, her eyes still on Willard's.

"Yes?"

"Pamela?" She recognized the voice of Mitchell Marks.

"Yes, Mitchell. What's up?"

"I believe I have some information for you about the murder recording."

"Please don't tell me that the murderer sounds like Ballard," she said into the receiver.

"What?" said Marks, obviously confused.

"Never mind," she said, shaking her head, "I'm sorry, Mitchell. What information do you have?"

"You'd better come down here so I can show you." He hung up and Pamela was left holding the receiver. "Mitchell's figured out something about the recording too, Willard. He wants me to come down."

"Let's go," said Willard, turning and heading out the doorway. Pamela grabbed her keys and locking her door, followed Willard down the hallway and into the stairwell. When they reached the main floor, Willard waddled out into the hall with his cane, puffing with excitement. She managed to keep up.

They arrived to discover Jane Marie standing at Mitchell's doorway, talking to her boss. When Mitchell saw Pamela, he waved her into his office. Willard followed.

"Mitchell," explained Pamela, "Willard and I were just working on the recording when you called. He found something strange about the killer. His voice is almost identical to that of Ballard."

"No way!" said Mitchell. Pamela feared that Mitchell was going to declare that he had just discovered that the killer's voice was totally different from Ballard's and they'd really be at an impasse. However, Mitchell had a totally different finding. He led Pamela and Willard over to his computer monitor and hit the play button.

"Listen," he said, "to the gunshot and listen to what happens after the gunshot."

They listened as directed to the recording that they had now heard dozens if not hundreds of times. Mitchell motioned for them to sit in the chairs in front of his desk and they quickly took their places, their ears following the sound track of the murder.

"Pamela," Mitchell said, "I told you the other day, that there was something strange about the gunshot. I couldn't figure it out, but now I believe I can say what's not happening—even if I can't say what is happening. Let me explain. We're assuming Ballard is sitting directly behind the mic and the killer is standing in the doorway."

"Yes," said Pamela. "I took those measurements. The doorway is about ten feet from the microphone. However, I should tell you that Detective Shoop called me yesterday to tell me that the autopsy report indicated that the bullet entry came from below. So, the killer must have either been sitting or kneeling or else very short. I still can't figure that out."

"It doesn't make sense to me either. But let me tell you what I'm hearing. If the killer shoots the gun from the door and the bullet hits Ballard at the microphone, we should hear—I think—less sound from the gunshot and more sound from the impact of the bullet—it would all happen almost instantaneously. Certainly with Ballard at the mic we would hear bullet impact and some sound from Ballard when he's hit—after all he's sitting directly in front of the mic. But we don't hear any of that. We hear the gunshot and then nothing."

"I thought about that too, Mitchell," she said, "but it doesn't make sense."

"I know," Mitchell agreed, "We hear the gunshot and then someone seems to turn off the microphone and shuts off the power and it happens within a few seconds. I'm assuming it must be the killer. But if it were, wouldn't you hear the killer walking towards the mic—even faintly?"

"It's true," added Willard, "we can hear the killer vocalize when we assume he brings out the gun. Surely, even if he were wearing soft shoes, we'd hear some sound as he walked towards the microphone."

"My students in my acoustics seminar noted this too, Willard," she added. "Gentlemen, I don't know what this means, but you can bet I'm going to find out."

Chapter 26

Previous week--December 15-16, late Saturday night—early Sunday morning

David Bridgewater, alias Ted Ballard, entered the front door of radio station KRDN around 11:30 p.m. Saturday night. Carl Edwards was still on-air and greeted him as his gave his spiel into the microphone. David took off his overcoat and wandered over to the CD collections behind Edwards and started searching for songs he might play for his program that night. He carried several CDs that he replaced in the station's music library.

When Edwards started a tune playing, he leaned back in his chair and spoke to David.

"Hey, Ted, you're looking spiffy tonight. Got a date later?"

"Nah," replied David, "been getting some flack from my advisor. She says I have to look more presentable for my classes."

"Yeah," said the disc jockey, rising and walking to get a cup of coffee from an automatic pot on a nearby table, "I guess that would make me feel obligated to get a hair cut too."

"I feel bald," said David, rolling his eyes.

"You look truly middle class, buddy," said Edwards, patting David on the back and returning to his desk with his paper cup of java.

"Thanks," replied David.

"Hey," Edwards called out. "I'm setting up a series of about five songs. Can you sign off for me so I can get out of here?"

"Sure," said David, "take off."

"Thanks, pal," replied Edwards as he pre-set several songs in order and grandly polished the desk chair with his elbow before bowing in front of David. David laughed and sat down and put up his feet, noticing that there were at least ten minutes left of play time to run. "I'm taking off. See ya!" said Edwards.

Edwards grabbed his coat from the rack near the front of the studio and wrapped a warm scarf over his ear muffs before heading out into the cold night. David waved at his exiting form. A minute or so later, Edwards' car had disappeared from the front of the building and David, checking to see that there was still sufficient play time, grabbed his coat and quickly zipped outside and opened his trunk. He extracted a large shopping bag, closed the trunk, and returned into the studio. After taking off his coat, he took the bag to the disc jockey's console and set it in front of him. He peeked inside and reached in among a variety of objects, finally extracting one object he was searching for at the bottom.

The object was a black hand gun. After looking at the gun, opening it and checking to be certain that it was loaded, David placed the weapon in the right hand pocket of his black trousers. He tugged the pants around and glanced down to be certain that the bulge from the gun was not noticeable. Then he placed the shopping bag under the console and sat at the chair.

Soon the music that Edwards had set in motion was finished and David had to announce that his program—Black Vulture's program was starting a bit early. He immediately played Calliope Doom's latest song—Cursed Bones—a long one that he knew would play for quite a while. Glancing at his watch, he realized that it was now midnight. Saturday had turned to Sunday. The real show was about to begin. The stage was set and the main actor was in position. All that was needed now, he thought, was the rest of the cast. However, in this particular show, the rest of the cast didn't realize they were part of the show.

Calliope Doom's grinding metallic beat throbbed away confirming the intensity of David's feelings and the determination of his motivation. He was ready. Show time. To hell with writing dissertations, teaching, and being a small town disc jockey any longer. His life was about to change. All he had to do was perform his part to perfection—something he was sure he could do.

The music concluded and he flipped the on-air mic. "Okay, folks out there in radio land," he began, "that was Calliope's Doom with Cursed Bones." He rattled on about the alternative rock group and various other groups and songs that he was recommending. He threw in a commercial for "Avery's Auto Repair" on South Jackson and even suggested that local college students get their cars tuned up before heading home for Christmas break. He started to set up another song from Ochre Fugue that he'd heard on one of his forays to New Orleans.

Headlights from a car shone through the tall glass windows of the studio and a car's engine sounded as it pulled in front of the station. David speculated as to who his visitor might be this late at night in such an isolated location. He continued to give his audience a running commentary of the mysterious visitor as the person entered the studio.

As his brother Daniel walked in the front door of the studio and saw David sitting at the console, he smiled. David was talking into a large microphone sitting on the desk, greeting him for all his listeners to hear. Daniel felt somewhat uncomfortable in being an unseen center of attention.

"Oh, hi! Come on in!" said David to his brother. Daniel stepped inside the small studio and shut the door. "I'm Theodore Ballard—Black Vulture to my fans. You a fan of alternative rock?" rattled on David, confusing Daniel. How strange, he thought. David knows who I am; he invited me here.

Then David pulled a gun from his pocket and pointed it at Daniel's head. Daniel gasped.

"What the? That's a gun! What do you need a gun for? Why are you pointing it at me? Wha--? No! No!" said David. Daniel was totally confused and disoriented. Why was his brother holding a gun on him and speaking as if it was he who was holding the gun on him? Then David pulled the trigger and Daniel fell to the ground.

As soon as Daniel hit the floor, David leaped into action. He immediately turned off the microphone. Then he removed the shopping bag from beneath the console. He took it over to Daniel, now lying on the ground in front of the entrance door. A small bloody hole marred his otherwise serene face. David checked Daniel's neck for a pulse and found none. Quickly, David removed his own clothes and then Daniel's clothes—starting with David's overcoat. He fingered Daniel's coat pocket and found his car keys. Setting the coat and keys aside, he pulled on Daniel's neat chinos and button-down cotton shirt. He slipped into his brown loafers. Dressing in Daniel's clothes was easy; getting Daniel into his clothes was much harder. He tugged his tight black trousers over Daniel's legs and up his hips. Daniel weighed about the same as he did, but the trousers were tight on him too. It was difficult getting his black shirt that was decorated with a lovely blood covered rose and a saber onto his brother—there were so many buttons. The hardest part was getting Daniel's feet into his high black boots and tying them.

Then, from the shopping bag, David pulled out hair wax, a brush, a comb and hair spray. He quickly went to work making Daniel's hair have that sexy, romantic Goth look, complete with spikes, and points. He even had an eyebrow pencil which he used to line Daniel's eyes for that extra touch. As he was working on his dead brother, he realized that the bullet that had killed him was still lodged in his head. All for the best, he thought. If it had left his skull and lodged somewhere in the wall, he'd be forced to find it and retrieve it. He couldn't afford to leave any evidence that would point to Daniel's true identity. When he'd finished making the switch—one brother for another—he dragged Daniel's body from in front of the station door to behind the console and arranged it to look as if Daniel had been seated and had fallen out of the chair when he was shot.

"Sorry, Danny Boy," David said to the dead man at his feet, "nothing personal. Just a perfect solution to an otherwise insolvable problem." He pulled his wallet from his back pocket and switched it with Daniel's wallet. Then, he carefully scoured the floor and the surrounding area for any trace of the crime, depositing anything he found in his shopping bag, When he was assured that he had accounted for every possible eventuality, he grabbed Daniel's coat and car keys and headed outside where he took off in Daniel's Acura leaving his old beat-up Ford pick-up in the station's parking lot. The whole episode had taken approximately ten minutes.

Chapter 27

Present time--December 21, Friday evening

She never thought she'd find herself on a double date with her daughter, but that was exactly where she was. After meeting with Willard and Mitchell and getting inspired with their new leads on the clues on the murder recording, she had returned to her office to continue working on her analysis—only to be interrupted by Kent. When she engaged her assistant in a conversation about the musical proclivities of the recently deceased disc jockey, he informed her that there was a major alternative rock event going on Friday night in New Orleans—a so-called underground vampire ball. Kent told her that many alternative rock musicians who Ted Ballard had endorsed would be playing at some of the highly touted concerts and that he was planning on attending. In fact, he had invited her daughter to accompany him and she had agreed. As Pamela continued to prod Kent for information about the event, she discovered that it was not one event, but a multitude of events happening in various locations in the French Quarter. Although the ball was well organized and advertised, it was not "official" in the respect that there were any public notices. According to Kent, you had to be "in the know" to realize it was going on, and to get invited. He was one of the lucky ones. After additional poking and suggesting, Pamela managed to finagle an invitation from the young man for herself and Rocky. It would be like a "double date" she explained, wondering if he was even aware of this term. When Pamela informed Rocky that they would be going with Angela and Kent on their date to the underground vampire ball in New Orleans, Rocky was torn between fury (at his wife for planning his weekend before checking, and relief that he would be able to keep tabs on his daughter while she was in what he considered one of the most dangerous places on earth).

Now, here they all were—all four of them, together--seated around a small round, metal-topped table in an even smaller bar in the Quarter. The smoke level was worse than the sound level—and that was more from the people talking than from the music. The music was bad enough, thought Pamela. She looked at Rocky, who cringed in response to her sheepish smile. Angela ignored them—she'd been ignoring them all evening—embarrassed beyond belief to have her parents chaperoning her date. Kent was totally involved with the band on the small stage across from the bar. He and Angela didn't stand out too much as there were actually some customers dressed like the two young students were. No one was dressed like Rocky and Pamela, however. Many of the patrons were costumed—or, at least, Pamela hoped they were costumes—as vampires or other creatures she imagined were from vampire lore.

As she peeked over her left shoulder, a tall man with shiny long, black hair and a red velvet tuxedo jacket, was drinking some sort of blood-looking drink (hopefully tomato juice) and waxing eloquent to his partner (Pamela guessed she was female) who was dressed in a flowing black chiffon gown. Her long black tresses reached the middle of her back and her stark red lipstick and intense dark lashes popped against her chalk-white skin. Both of the lovers sported fangs proudly, smiling for Pamela whenever she ventured to glance their way.

"Just keep your eyes to yourself, Mom," repeated Angela to her mother under her breath, "You're gawking. It's not polite."

"I don't see vampires every day," responded Pamela, giving her daughter a sweet smile.

"What do you expect at the Vampire's Ball?" whispered Rocky. Was he enjoying her discomfort? He was livid about even having to come here in the first place. Of course, he had purchased some strange alcoholic concoction for the two of them. She was sipping hers but Rocky had slurped his down with gusto. "I'm going to get another of these," he announced, and headed towards the bar.

"Dr. B," said Kent, turning around towards her, "Listen to this next group. This is one of the bands that Ted Ballard was sponsoring. He played their first album on his show. Maybe after their set we can try to talk to them."

Good idea, thought Pamela. We need to do something to justify coming all the way down to New Orleans. So far, she hadn't learned anything that she thought would explain anything more about Ted Ballard or who might have wanted him dead.

A tall man wearing a long black cape floated onto the stage, swooping his cape around in dramatic bull-fighting waves. He stopped before the microphone and spoke to the audience, "Welcome, humans and lovers of the night. We here at the Black Rose are honored that you have decided to join us in your revelry. The band you just heard was Calliope's Doom—music you can sink your teeth into." He smirked, exposing two very white fangs. His entire demeanor gave Pamela the creeps. Angela smiled benignly and Kent nodded. The vampire Master of Ceremony gazed out at the audience and slowly ran his tongue around his lips. "Our next group is Pandemonium Passion. Let's give them a warm, wet, bloody welcome." He demonstrated a sharp applause and the audience followed. Then he lifted his cape and swirled it around before exiting through a curtained door in the back wall. Pandemonium Passion trudged out on stage. The five musicians were all in black. Surprise, thought Pamela. Now, she wondered, will they or won't they have fangs? That's about the only question left. As she stared at the group, Rocky returned to their table, no drink in hand. He sat down and bent to her ear, speaking with agitation.

"I'm not sure. It's really dark, but I'd swear that's Ted Ballard sitting at the bar."

"What?" gasped Pamela. "Where?" Rocky attempted to discreetly point at a man seated alone. He was wearing jeans and a simple t-shirt. "Kent," she whispered to the young man at her table, gesturing for him to come closer, "Does that man sitting alone at the bar look like Ted Ballard to you?"

"What do you mean, look like him?" asked Kent, peering around Pamela, attempting to get a view of the man in question.

"Mom," said Angela, "you're making a scene. People are trying to listen to the band."

"Sorry, honey," said Pamela, "I just need to know if Kent recognizes someone."

"I can't tell, Dr. B," said Kent, "He's turned away."

"I may be wrong," said Rocky, "I just remember him from seeing him in Trudi's office from time to time. It can't be him, obviously. But it really looks like him."

"Let me check," said Kent.

"Wait!" said Pamela, "What if he recognizes you?"

"Dr. B," explained Kent, "What's there to recognize? It can't be Ballard. He's dead. It's probably just someone who looks like him. Let me check him out. I'll be careful—and casual. I promise." Without waiting for her answer, Kent rose from the table and wove his way through the crowd, past the man at the bar and went into the men's room.

"Now where's he going?" whispered Pamela, following the young man with her eyes.

"You told him to be discreet," said Rocky, pulling on her arm, "He's just following directions. Calm down."

"You two are driving me crazy!" exclaimed Angela, glaring at her parents. "I knew this was a ridiculous idea! I've never been so embarrassed in my life!"

As Pamela looked up, she saw Kent weaving his way back from the restroom. He reached their table and dropped into his chair beside Angela. "Hey, Ang, miss me?" he quizzed the young woman who scowled at him. He chuckled and gave her shoulders a squeeze.

"Did you get a look at him?" asked Pamela.

"He really kind of looks like Ballard, doesn't he?" asked Rocky, seeming to need validation for his original identification.

"He doesn't just look like Ballard," said Kent, causing Rocky to deflate, "he is Ballard." Kent let his words sink in around the table.

"You mean he looks like Ballard," said Pamela.

"No," said Kent, "I've seen Ballard at clubs, many times. Even up close. This man is a little neater than Ballard usually looks, but it's him. I'd swear to it."

"How can that be?" asked Angela. "The guy is dead."

"I know," said Kent. "It doesn't make any sense."

"I can't explain it either," ventured Pamela, "but whether he is Ballard or just really looks like Ballard, our predicament is the same."

"How?" asked Kent and Angela.

"I think she means that we have to do something," said Rocky, "I mean, we're obligated to contact the police. Let them figure out the significance of this man—whether or not it is Ballard."

"We can't just go up to him and suggest he go to the police," said Kent.

"And I don't think we'd better attempt to talk to him," added Pamela. "I mean, there may be a perfectly innocuous reason for this seeming clone of Ballard, and if we approach him, maybe he'd respond to our request to explain or contact the police...."

"But maybe he won't," contradicted Rocky. "I'm more inclined to think there's something strange going on."

"So, Mom," said Angela, "you're the detective, what should we do?"

"We follow him and see where he goes."

"No," said Rocky, "that might prove to be dangerous. We're not the police. I say we contact the police and explain this to them and let them deal with it."

"Rocky," argued Pamela, "Just what in the world would we say to the New Orleans' police about this? We saw a guy in a bar who looks a lot like a guy who was murdered a few hundred miles away from here. We want you to come to this bar and question him?"

"I don't know," said Rocky, looking skeptical. The two couples sat quietly for a while looking around the table at each other, attempting to decide what to do about their dilemma. From the corner of his eye, Kent noticed the man at the bar, stand, throw a few dollars on the counter and head for the front exit.

"Oh, my god," said Kent, "he's leaving."

"Let's go," said Pamela, standing and starting out. Kent and Angela followed her immediately. Rocky, sighing, placed two twenty dollar bills on the table and followed the three of them towards the doorway.

Chapter 28

Previous week--December 16, early Sunday morning

Daniel's Acura was certainly a better car than David was used to driving. He was heading south, away from the center of what he knew would soon become a major crime scene. With luck, they wouldn't discover the body until the morning when the next disc jockey was scheduled to arrive. If he was unlucky and anyone was actually listening to his show, they might report the gun shot and the resultant end of the program to the police. That might cause things to move faster. If it did, the sooner he got out of Reardon, the better. Immediately after he left KRDN, he drove over to the motel where he knew Daniel was registered, went to his room which he figured out from the hotel key in his wallet. In the hotel room, he cleared out any evidence of Daniel's stay and carefully wiped away any finger prints that he (David) might have left. Luckily, Daniel had several hundred dollars in his wallet as well as two or three credit cards. He checked out of the hotel, signing the register in Daniel's name.

As soon as he was outside of Reardon and on the road, he drove for several hours until, exhausted he stopped for the night at a small out of the way hotel off the Interstate. He slept for a few hours and left around 8 a.m., after a quick breakfast, paying with cash. On the road again, he used Daniel's iPhone to make a few important calls. He started with the most innocuous. He called the Bridgewater Carpet company switchboard and listened to the answering machine just to get a feel for the old place. Then, after practicing Daniel's voice out loud—he felt he'd heard him speak enough during their few hours together—he called Harold Vickers, the family lawyer. Daniel had made it clear to him that Harold was aware of his trip and Daniel appeared to update Harold regularly with reports on his progress in bringing David home. He also called Harold to get reports on his father's condition. David knew that he would have to maintain this behavior in order to convince Vickers that he was Daniel.

He pressed the number on the iPhone listed for Vickers. The man came on the line.

"Daniel," said the older man, "how's it going? Did you convince him to return yet?"

"Harold," greeted David in his new voice, "I'm working on it. Unfortunately, David seems to be embroiled in the middle of some problems of his own that are taking up quite a bit of his time."

"Really?"

"Yeah," explained David, "I don't know what it is exactly, but he's all involved with some weird characters—tattoos, rock bands, drugs, that stuff. I'm afraid maybe he's in over his head. Like, maybe he owes money or something. I couldn't get a lot out of him."

"You didn't tell me that," said Vickers, concerned. "Should I come over there? Maybe I can help. If it's money...."

"No, no!" said David, quickly. "Um, don't do that. I'm not even sure that's the problem. It may be something else—like a woman—or drugs. He's not terribly talkative. You know, very reserved."

"Okay," agreed Vickers, "if you think that's best, but I can be there. I can wire as much as you need."

"It's fine, Harold," said David, "but, let's take this one step at a time. I don't want to scare him off. I've got at least a dialogue going with him. How's--father?"

"Same," said Harold. "No change. Which, I guess, you can look at as good."

"Yeah," replied David, hiding his disappointment, "Well, I'm going to keep working on him. I'll be checking with you. Just let me handle things here my own way, okay?"

"Sure," agreed Vickers, "and I'll give your best to your father."

"Uh, yes," said David, "please give Father my best wishes." He grimaced, trying to keep the disgust he was feeling out of his voice.

David clicked off the line and continued driving. That was close. All he needed was that supercilious, over-attentive attorney mucking things up. Even so, the call had gone relatively well. He'd planted the seed he needed. When the murder hit the news—and it would probably hit the news sooner than later, he'd be ready for it.

The mileage sign on his right announced, "New Orleans 230 miles." He knew this road well as he'd spent much time in the Big Easy. He even knew the perfect little out of the way bed and breakfast in the Quarter where he could stay—no questions asked. He knew the owner—a well-endowed middle aged woman with red hair—not just auburn, but red—like a fire truck. Just thinking about Melba and her attributes made him anticipate what he figured would be his last trip to New Orleans in a long, long time. However long it would be before he returned to his favorite town in the world would be too long. He would have to make this trip, worth the effort, even though it would, of necessity, be low-key.

He had a lot to accomplish. He didn't know how much time he had; it all depended on his father. This was the one feature of his plan on which he had no control. With luck, the old man would kick the bucket sooner rather than later. But, Daniel had assured him that their father was dying and it was just a matter of waiting. Staying out of sight, until the old man was dead. He could do that. He could do that quite well in NOLA, where he knew the people and the locale. And while he was waiting, he had things to prepare—many things to prepare.

Not long now. The mileage sign said "New Orleans 180 miles."

He didn't call anyone else on Daniel's iPhone—even though there were dozens of names listed—including #4 for an "Amy." He figured she was probably one of Danny Boy's main squeezes as were some of the other names listed by first name only. Around 9 a.m., when David heard

Daniel's iPhone ring, he picked it up and looked at the caller ID which indicated "Amy" was calling.

"No way, Danny Boy," he said to the iPhone, "I'm not going to be chatting with your girl friends. They'll just have to find another easy touch." He slipped the iPhone back in his pocket and continued driving.

After receiving no response to several calls to Dan's iPhone, Amy was getting terribly worried and decided to call Harold Vickers. After all, Dan had told her he'd told Vickers about their relationship and if she had any problems, she should call him. She still had that bug and she was sitting on the floor of her bathroom, her head over the toilet. Between rounds of vomiting, she called Vickers on her cell phone. When he answered, she cautiously told him who she was and informed Vickers that Daniel wasn't answering his phone and she was worried.

"Amy," said the kind sounding man, "I wouldn't worry. Daniel just called me a while ago. He's still working on David, although there are some problems—on David's end—some problems David's having that are keeping him busy and that Daniel believes are interfering with his ability to get David to return home. I figure he's just embroiled in this personal mess of David's. That's probably why he's not returning your call. He's probably right in the middle of things over there."

"You're probably right," agreed Amy, "It's so like Dan to try to help his brother out of a jam. Does David need money, is that it?

"I asked him that and he said no," replied Vickers. "Let's just let him work on David in his own way for a while. I'm sure we'll hear from him when he has something to report."

"Okay," said Amy, not as assured as she would like to be. "It's a relief to know that you spoke with him."

"Yes, I did," said Vickers, "and he sounded fine. But, he told me about you...so, I understand why you're concerned."

"Thanks," she said, "But if I don't hear from him pretty soon, you'll be hearing from me again."

"And I want to hear from you. Take care, Amy. I'm on your side. Yours and Daniel's." Then he clicked off.

Amy tried to feel reassured by the fact that Vickers had just spoken to Dan, but she couldn't help but wonder why Dan would call his lawyer and not his wife.

Chapter 29

Present time--December 22, Saturday

Pamela, Rocky, Angela, and Kent had arrived back in Reardon late the previous night—frustrated. They had tried to follow the person they thought was Ted Ballard—or who looked a lot like Ted Ballard. They had chased him around the streets of the French Quarter as he visited several bars involved in the vampire underground ball—each one more flamboyant than the next. The Ballard clone walked around each location, sometimes greeting people, sometimes ordering and consuming a drink. This went on until about 2:00 in the morning when the four detectives followed him to an Acura parked on a side street. The man got into the car, started driving quickly through the winding side streets of the Quarter and then, almost as if in a magician's act—disappeared.

Rocky drove around several blocks again and again while the four of them looked for the man, but it was to no avail. He had disappeared and they had to admit defeat, give up and return home. They eventually returned to Reardon around 4:00 a.m. on Saturday morning. Kent had parked his car at the Barnes' house and he left with a quick farewell to Angela and her parents. Then the Barnes' family entered their home, discouraged and demoralized because they had failed in their efforts.

They all three—Pamela, Rocky, and Angela—slept late. Even Candide seemed to realize that his family had been through the ringer and allowed them all to stay in bed without his usual 6 a.m. wake-up call. It was after noon when Pamela finally opened one lid a mite and saw sunlight streaming in from her bedroom window. She rolled her head around to focus in on her digital clock which gleamed back "12:43 p.m." in seeming accusation.

She took a deep breath and dragged her feet over the edge of the bed and into her awaiting slippers. Grabbing her tericloth robe from the chair by the dresser she wrapped herself in its warmth and headed out to the kitchen. Candide greeted her from his bed in the kitchen and nipped at her legs demanding his breakfast. A dog's breakfast, thought Pamela, now there's a meal I'm qualified to make, as she scooped some of her poodle's favorite kibble into his bowl and replaced his water. Her pet was satisfied but she was anything but. All that work last night trying to find that man that Kent and her husband were certain was a perfect match for the dead disc jockey. They had driven all over the French Quarter with no luck. He could be anywhere, she realized. And what if they'd found him? What would they do? Ask him why he looked like the dead Ted Ballard? None of what happened last night made any sense to Pamela.

She thought back to her sound analysis. She was certain that the killer's acoustic profile indicated that the killer was an educated, Southern male. She was certain that there was something strange about the actual gun shot. According to Mitchell, the initial explosion was too loud and there was no apparent impact sound—certainly, there was no sound from Ballard when he was hit by the bullet. Then, just a few seconds and the microphone was turned off—apparently. If the killer walked over to the mic and turned it off, there was no sound of his footsteps. She realized that the murder scene that she was envisioning in her head—the scene that was established in the dj's monologue—was not actually supported by the sounds on the recording. Hmm. She was making assumptions, she thought to herself. They were all making assumptions--all based on what the disc jockey said on air.

She opened her bag of select espresso blend that she liked to drink on Sunday mornings when she had more time to savor it. She filled the filter to the brim, knowing that Rocky would want coffee too when he woke up. Heavens, even

Angela might want coffee after the night they all had. She placed the filter in the pot, filled the upper container with water, and hit *brew*. Realizing that she was the only one in the family awake, she decided to attempt making breakfast. How hard could it be? Reaching above the stove where Rocky stored his cookbooks, she grabbed a particularly used-looking one and used the tabs to find the section on "Breakfasts." Opening the book and placing it on the kitchen counter, she located a recipe that looked relatively easy and started gathering the necessary ingredients.

As she worked, she thought again about the assumptions she was making about the disc jockey's murder. She had assumed—they all had assumed-- that the killer entered the studio door, remained at the door, shot the dj who was seated at the desk, walked to the desk, turned off the microphone, and then exited. Maybe that was not what actually happened. She poured flour into her large bowl. It did not flow out smoothly from the sack and a puff of flour exploded into her face. She wiped the white powder from her eyes and mouth and barreled ahead. If the gun shot was loud for the initial explosion but softer for impact, maybe the killer and victim had somehow exchanged positions. But how? And why? She wondered. Why would the killer sit at the microphone and the victim walk to the door? That scenario didn't make sense. Well, at least it didn't make sense according to what they knew was happening from what the disc jockey said.

She cracked an egg into the flour, added a cup of milk, and started stirring the thin liquid. Unfortunately, her mixing bowl wasn't large enough for all the ingredients she was using, and large amounts of the mixture poured over the top of the bowl onto the counter and eventually onto the floor. Hmm, she thought. Cooking is such a messy activity. Maybe the problem was that they were all assuming that what they were hearing on the recording—that is, what Ted Ballard was saying--was an accurate representation of what actually happened. She added a spoonful of vanilla which dribbled onto her fingers, causing her to lick the tips. Not bad. She turned to the stove and extracted the large flat griddle from beneath the oven. She placed it on the largest burner, turned on the gas, and plopped a glob of butter on the surface. The butter sizzled and she grabbed a plastic cup and dipped it into the pancake mixture. As she brought it up to pour on the griddle, droplets of mixture trailed all the way from the counter to the stove and onto her slippers. Ick! How does Rocky do this and stay so neat? she wondered. Lucky for Ballard's killer that he used a handgun because it wasn't very messy. The bullet remained lodged in his brain, according to the autopsy. There was very little blood. But that still doesn't account for the discrepancies in the sound. The only thing that would account for the sound being loud at the mic and soft at the door would be, she realized, if the killer was seated at the desk and the victim was standing at the door. In fact, she realized immediately, that such a repositioning would also account for the strange angle of entry of the bullet—the bullet coming from below rather than straight or from above. Let me think this through, she said to herself, as she flung another cup-full of pancake batter on the stove. She took a spatula and peeked under her first cake. Ooops! A little too done, she realized as she attempted to flip it. Too bad! It ripped in half, leaving one part stuck to the griddle and the other half now resting on top. A lost cause, she realized as scraped her first attempt off the griddle and dumped it in the waste basket. She resolved to keep a better eye on the second pancake.

Watching a second pancake—and a third and a fourth—with an eagle eye, she hovered over the stove. If, she thought, the killer was seated at the desk in front of the mic and the victim were standing by the door—all of the clues fit. The gun blast would be loud because it occurred immediately in front of the microphone. We don't hear the bullet impact because it's further away, by the door. We also don't hear any sound from the victim on impact because the victim is too far from the mic. The angle of bullet entry would be right too, she realized because if the killer was seated at the desk and the victim was standing, that would create a wound with the bullet entering from below. She flipped her three pancakes. One of the three made the journey unscathed.

This new scenario, she realized, also could explain the reason the mic was turned off so fast and why they heard no footsteps. If the killer was seated at the desk, he merely reached over and flipped off the microphone. He didn't have to walk to the desk from the door. It all fit, she thought. She piled the three lop-sided little cakes on a platter and started on a new set with three new cupfuls of batter. These would be better, she vowed. All of the acoustic and physical evidence worked with her new scenario of having the killer at the desk and the victim standing—all except the recording. The recording seemed to indicate the exact opposite. The only reason she could see for the recording to be wrong would be if the killer somehow plotted to make it that way. But if he did, how did he do it? And how did he get Ballard to change places with him and make the tape? There were still so many questions. If she didn't know any better, she would think that Ballard had masterminded his own murder, because everything with this new scenario seemed to implicate the seated person—by all rights—the disc jockey, as the killer. But, the disc jockey—Ballard--was dead. He didn't kill himself, obviously. Or, did he?

She opened the refrigerator and got out syrup and some bacon. She'd have to keep thinking about the murder—the recording and the clues. Somehow or other they would point her in the right direction. She placed the syrup on the table and started the bacon. She got plates and silverware from the cupboards and set the table. As the bacon hit the frying pan, Candide set up a tirade of barking when the odor of cooking pork hit the air. Two bodies appeared in the kitchen door.

"My god, Mom," yawned Angela, in her *de rigeur* bedspread, "what are you doing?"

"Making breakfast," Pamela responded brightly, holding up her spatula as a badge of honor, pancake batter dripping from her hair and robe.

"At least you didn't burn down the house this time," grumbled Rocky. Then he smiled and walked over and gave her a kiss on the cheek.

Chapter 30

Previous week--December 17, Monday

David Bridgewater had found an out of the way small bed and breakfast on a side street of the French Quarter. Here he had holed up as he prepared for the next phase of his project and waited for the call that he hoped would come soon, but that he knew would come eventually. His look had changed. He had now transformed into a traditional, conventional, young businessman. His hair was trimmed neatly—no facial hair remained. He had purchased a wardrobe of comparable clothing to add to what he had already changed into from his brother's dead body. He had discarded all of Daniel's personal items and his suitcase in various trash bins around New Orleans. He was careful to remove any identification and to not deposit too many items in the same place. He remained very low key. The only pleasure he allowed himself during this time of–what he considered—transition were nightly visits to some of his favorite alternate music bars. He realized he probably stuck out in his new attire, but he speculated that people would just think he was a tourist trying to pick up some local color. Also, as he knew that the underground vampire ball was in full swing in the next few days, he was anxious to take in some of his favorite bands—some he'd introduced on air himself and had helped get their start.

He realized that the news of "Theodore Ballard's death" might create some problems for him. After all, his brother had found him so people knew where he was. That private dick Danny Boy had hired knew his alias, so he—or anyone he or Daniel may have mentioned the name Ted Ballard to— might become suspicious if—when—the news of "Ballard's" death got out. Hopefully, it wouldn't reach his family or their entourage—and if so—no one would connect the news of Ballard's death to David Bridgewater—wayward son. If it did, he was ready with a cover story.

He kept getting calls from Daniel's obnoxious girlfriend Amy. You'd think she'd give up; he'd ignored all her calls. Surely, she'd get the message that he wasn't interested. The last thing he needed was some clingy, uptight society daughter looking to hook herself a Bridgewater. She might have gotten her clutches into Danny Boy, but not him. David knew what he intended to do with the Bridgewater fortune—once it was his and he didn't intend to share it with anyone.

Amy was frustrated beyond belief. Daniel was simply refusing to answer his phone. That must be it. Harold Vickers had spoken to him. According to Vickers, Dan had answered his phone and spoken with him. Vickers even asked Amy if she wanted him to ask Dan to call her, but she said she didn't. If he didn't want to talk to her, she'd deal with it herself. She didn't need a lawyer acting as a go-between for them. Besides, right now, talking to Dan wasn't even at the top of her list. She was still feeling terrible and she'd made an appointment with her doctor for this morning—if she could make it there without vomiting. She maneuvered her small car into a spot in front of her doctor's little clinic. She knew she could see Dr. Knowles, the Bridgewater family physician; Daniel had told her to go to him, but she just felt more comfortable with Dr. Lucy who she'd known for years.

Monday morning she assumed would find Dr. Lucy's waiting room packed, but amazingly it was empty except for Sherry, Dr. Lucy's receptionist/nurse. It was a very small practice and the large, motherly Sherry did everything that Dr. Lucy didn't do and then some.

"Miss Amy Shuster," Sherry cried, hugging Amy and patting her back like a mother burping an infant, "I haven't seen you in—years!"

"That's not true, Sherry. You know I'm here every year for my physical."

"Have you been hiding out?" Sherry's eyes looked her up and down, suspiciously.

"No," replied Amy, surprised, "I've just been busy with work."

"And what is wrong today?" asked Sherry, ever the professional as she escorted Amy directly into the back and into an examining room.

"I've got some bug, I think. I've been vomiting off and on for days. I'm exhausted."

"Dr. Lucy," said Sherry as an older woman with a long grey braid and warm brown eyes entered the room. She wore a stethoscope and carried a clip board. She smiled immediately when she saw Amy.

"So," said Dr. Lucy, her piercing eyes glancing over the young patient from head to toe, "you look a little peaked."

"Peaked," repeated Amy, "Is that a medical term?"

"No," replied Dr. Lucy, "but it describes how you look perfectly. Now, hop on the table and tell me what's wrong."

Amy complied and Dr. Lucy talked and asked questions of the young woman as she conducted a thorough physical exam, including blood work.

"Amy," she said, sitting on the chair beside the table, "I can't say for certain. I will need to wait for confirmation from the lab, but I believe I know the cause of your symptoms."

"What?" asked Amy.

"I hope I'm not adding to your problems," she said, taking Amy's hands, "but, my dear, it appears you're pregnant."

Chapter 31

Present time--Saturday, December 22, afternoon

"Detective Shoop," said Pamela when she finally got the police man on her phone, "Something strange has happened. Last night, my husband, my daughter, my graduate assistant and I went to New Orleans to do some background research on the alternative music scene. You know, the type of music played by Ted Ballard on his radio show."

"I know, Dr. Barnes," replied Shoop, "And I see you're out on your own detecting again. Didn't I warn you about that?"

"Yes, Detective," replied Pamela, "we were merely visiting some local music spots and listening to some of the local bands. I'd hardly call that dangerous."

"If," said Shoop, pointedly, "that's all you did. I assume you aren't calling me just to tell me you listened to some bands."

"No," she said, "while we were in one bar, we saw a man who resembled Ted Ballard, the murdered disc jockey. I mean, Detective, he more than resembled Ballard, actually. He was a dead ringer for the man."

"And you would know this, Dr. Barnes," added Shoop, "because you were so close to the man?" Shoop was always so skeptical.

"No," answered Pamela, "I wasn't, but my husband knew him from the English Department and my grad student knew him from the music scene. He'd run across him often at various rock performances—both in Reardon and in New Orleans."

"So, you're saying you saw someone who looked like Ballard?" asked Shoop calmly.

"Identical," she replied. "Identical."

Shoop remained quiet for a few moments. Pamela could almost hear him thinking over the phone.

"Actually, Dr. Barnes," he said, "Your discovery may have a simple explanation. There are some people I'd like you to meet. Could you possibly come down to the police station?"

"Now?"

"Yes, now," he replied, "I can't ask them to remain here indefinitely."

"I suppose so. Does this have something to do with the man we saw?"

"Maybe," replied Shoop, "just get down here." He hung up.

Pamela remained standing with the receiver in her hand, a puzzled look on her face. Rocky glared at her.

"What did he say?" he asked "What did he think when you told him about the guy that looks just like Ballard?"

"He says there's a simple explanation. He wants us to come down to the station and meet some people."

"What?"

"I don't know," she said to her husband. "Evidently, he thinks the man we chased and these people are connected. I'm going." She placed the receiver back on the phone base and headed for the bedroom. Quickly she started changing from nightgown, robe, and slippers to trousers, shirt, and shoes.

"You're not going alone," said Rocky, joining her in the competition to get dressed. "Who knows what that man wants from you? Maybe he wants you to identify a suspect from a line-up. It could be dangerous."

"Maybe," she said, brightening, "Maybe they caught the killer!"

"Hurry up," he said. As soon as they were dressed, the couple headed for Rocky's Accord and set out for the Police Station in downtown Reardon. When they arrived they parked in the "visitor" lot and quickly headed into the front door of the large, two-story, ochre-colored brick building. At the main desk, a uniformed officer directed them to

Shoop's office through a central section and towards the back of the building on the left. Pamela had been to Shoop's office several times before when she had assisted Shoop with the investigation into the murder of her colleague Charlotte Clark. As Pamela and Rocky reached the entrance to Shoop's office, they saw two people seated on chairs in front of the detective's desk—a young woman and an older man. Both carried winter coats over their arms. The young woman was crying. The older man had his arm around the young woman's shoulders protectively.

"Dr. Barnes, Mr. Barnes," Shoop said, standing at his desk as the couple entered. "I'd like you to meet Amy Shuster Bridgewater and Harold Vickers." All four people shook hands—for what reason they did not know—politely. Shoop brought over two chairs from the side of the office wall for Pamela and Rocky, had then sit down and closed his door. He then returned to the chair behind his desk.

"I realize," began Shoop, "that none of you know how the others are involved in all of this. Let me see if I can explain. Early last Sunday morning, a local disc jockey named Ted Ballard was shot to death while on air. We had no clues to the identity of the killer who seemed to vanish into thin air. Also, we had little information about or contacts for Ballard. I asked Dr. Barnes here," and he gestured towards Pamela, "to assist us with this investigation because we had a recording of the murder that the radio station had made and Dr. Barnes had been instrumental in solving a murder for us last year by analyzing a sound recording of a murder. She has been aiding us in our efforts. Dr. and Mr. Barnes, Mrs. Bridgewater and Mr. Vickers arrived in my office several hours ago and the tale they have brought me is astounding, I think you will believe. I believe, Dr. Barnes, you will see that it tells us the identity of the killer of Ted Ballard. Maybe, I'll let Mrs. Bridgewater tell you..."

"I don't think I...." said Amy, clasping a used handkerchief in her fist, tears welling up in her eyes.

"Let me, please," said Vickers. "Dr. Barnes, Mr. Barnes, I am the attorney for Charles Bridgewater, head of a well-known carpet-manufacturing family. Charles Bridgewater is dying. He has two sons, David and Daniel. Soon after high school graduation, David and his father got in a terrible feud. Charles disowned David and David left the family and the family hasn't heard from him since—which is how Charles claimed he wanted it. Daniel has been running the business since his father became ill, but Daniel has always wanted to reunite his father and his brother. With his father's impending death, Daniel felt much greater pressure to bring his family back together, so he hired a private investigator to track down his brother. The investigator was able to find David living under an assumed name..."

"Ted Ballard?" asked Pamela.

"You are three steps ahead of me," said Vickers. "Yes. When Daniel discovered where his brother was, he was determined to go to him and bring him home to try to make things right between him and his father before his father died. Daniel headed here and actually met with David. Things seemed to be going okay. Daniel was reporting to me regularly. He thought he would be able to convince his brother to return. He indicated to me that David wanted him to visit the radio station where David was a disc jockey. Daniel planned to go there last Saturday night which I assume he did. The next day, I heard from Daniel—or I thought it was Daniel--and he indicated that he was still having trouble convincing David and that David was having serious problems that he didn't know he'd be able to solve. He didn't indicate what those problems were, but I got the idea that he thought maybe he was into drugs or some type of crime. Then, Amy found what she did."

"I'm sorry, Dr. Barnes," said Amy, sniffling, "I know you've helped solve this whole mess, but for me, it's too late. Too late."

Vickers gave her shoulder a squeeze.

"I'm Dan's wife—actually his secret wife," said Amy proudly. "We've tried to keep our marriage secret because of all of this trauma going on about David and Dan's father. Dan wanted to tell his father about us; he was planning on telling him the minute he got David and his father back together. I worried that it might be dangerous for Dan to try to bring his brother back, but I never thought he'd be murdered."

"Murdered?" exclaimed Pamela.

"While Dan was on this wild goose chase to bring his brother home, he would report in to me regularly by phone—several times a day. He told me about his plans to see David—or Ted Ballard—perform at the radio station Saturday night. When he didn't call me the next day, I knew something was wrong. I called Harold and he said Dan was calling him regularly. It didn't make sense—all of a sudden he stops contacting his wife when he is calling his lawyer. I started to go crazy when he didn't respond. I even went online and looked up information for the station where David worked and the town and discovered to my horror that the disc jockey Ted Ballard that I knew was David Bridgewater had been murdered. I called Harold and we realized immediately that something horrible was wrong. We suspected that it was David who was calling him and not calling me. We contacted Detective Shoop because he was listed in the newspaper stories as the officer in charge. He suggested we come here and see if we could identify the body."

"Yes," continued Shoop, "Mrs. Bridgewater just identified her husband's body at the morgue. The person who was killed was not David Bridgewater—alias Ted Ballard. It was Daniel Bridgewater."

"Dan had several false upper teeth in a partial plate. He had a minor accident at the plant several years ago and kept it quiet for insurance reasons," Amy said softly, "He never wanted anyone to know. He didn't even like it that I knew about it. But when I told the coroner about the specific way the teeth were made, it seemed to verify that the victim was indeed Dan—not David."

"You see, Dr. Barnes, Mr. Barnes," continued Shoop, "The reason for the extreme confusion in the identification and the reason you thought you saw the dead Ted Ballard in New Orleans is that David and Daniel were identical twins."

"Identical twins," she gasped, "Now I see how he did it."

"You mean the murder recording?" asked Shoop.

"Yes," said Pamela, "the patter Ballard—or rather David--gives about the killer pointing the gun at him is all false. He's really pointing the gun at his brother, who is standing by the door. That's why we heard the brother gasp. Daniel was probably shocked to see his own brother pull a gun on him. And David shot him before he was able to respond. The angle of entry of the bullet matches because David was seated at the desk and Daniel was standing at the door. After David shot Daniel, he turned off the microphone. What happened after that I don't know."

"I can speculate," said Shoop, "He probably exchanged clothes with his brother, dragged the body to under the desk, took his wallet and keys, and left in his car. He then, no doubt, went to Daniel's hotel, checked out after clearing any trace of his brother from the hotel room, and headed for New Orleans where he was spotted by…"

"By us!" announced Rocky, triumphantly, "last night."

"All of this is fine," said Shoop, looking around the small office at the four people so intimately involved in this crime. "It appears we have identified the killer. Now we just have to catch him."

"And I know just how we can do that," said Vickers, holding up his cell phone and giving Amy a reassuring hug.

"How?" asked Shoop.

"We set a trap," replied Vickers. "Are you game?"

"I am!" exclaimed Pamela, and Rocky sighed, shaking his head.

Detective Shoop looked at Rocky, "I know just how you feel."

Chapter 32

Present time--December 23, Sunday

David Bridgewater rang the elaborate bell ringer on the massive door—totally unnecessary he surmised seeing as how this mansion was now his. He could just walk in. Oh well, I'll maintain decorum for a while, he thought. There was a death in the family, he reasoned. A certain degree of courtesy is called for. Plus, I'm not certain which of Danny Boy's keys fits the lock.

Harold Vickers answered the door.

"Daniel," he said, solemnly and gestured for David to enter. David walked into the spacious wood-paneled foyer of the Bridgewater mansion. "I'm so sorry about your father," continued Vickers. "I know it must be especially hard for you that you weren't here when he passed."

"Yes, Harold," replied David, "Very hard. Thank you for calling. Of course, we all knew it was only a matter of time. I'm only sorry I couldn't convince...David to come back before father passed. Are you serving as sentry now?"

"We've been receiving many condolence cards and packages," said Vickers, remaining standing. He was curious to see what David would do. It didn't matter if he decided to leave because, Vickers knew, Shoop had several officers stationed outside.

"Is the body at the mortuary?" asked David.

"No," replied Vickers, "Of course, we waited to have the body taken there because we knew you would want to say your good-byes in person."

"That wasn't necessary," replied David, slightly flushed. Not what he wanted. The less he saw of the old man, living or dead, the better.

"Fine," said David. "I'll just go up to my room and unpack and then I'll go see--father."

"I don't think you should wait, Daniel," said Vickers, urgently. "The mortuary would really like to proceed, so if you don't mind, you need to go directly to see your father."

"All right," agreed David, heading for the stairs. He couldn't make a fuss now or Vickers and the staff might suspect that he wasn't Daniel and that would never do. He headed up the long flight of carpet-covered stairs. Vickers followed behind like a retinue. At the head of the steps, he turned right, hoping that his father's bedroom would still be located in the same place. He figured if he walked into the wrong room he could claim he was disoriented due to grief. Opening the door at the end of the hallway, he was relieved to discover himself in his father's room. The old man's giant mahogany four-poster bed was located against one wall. The old man rested in the bed, the covers tucked under his chin, his eyes closed. He looked almost alive. Around the bed stood several people he didn't know—probably doctors and lawyers. He walked carefully towards the bed and when he arrived he sat on the edge of the bed, all the onlookers awaiting his reaction, obviously. The reaction they got was one of extreme shock, when suddenly his dead father opened his eyes.

"David," squeaked the old man, squeezing his eyes together to try to see his face.

What's going on? he thought, panicking. "Daniel, father," David gulped. Alive, he thought. The old man is supposed to be dead.

"No," said the old man, "David. You think I can't tell my own sons apart? Besides, how can you be Daniel, when Daniel is dead?"

David choked. What was going on? His father was alive. He knew he wasn't his brother. He knew Daniel was dead.

"I don't...."

"No...David," said Vickers, standing behind him. "I suppose you don't. But a lot of people have been working hard to find out who killed your brother—these people in this room to be exact." He pointed to Detective Shoop, Amy

Shuster Bridgewater, Rocky Barnes, and Pamela Barnes. "It was through their efforts that we know what you did to your own brother. That you killed him and attempted to pass yourself off for him. I assume that you thought that if your father were dead, you could get away with claiming you were Daniel and the entire Bridgewater fortune would be yours to do with as you pleased."

"You said he was dead," David retorted, pointing at the old man in the bed.

"I may be on my way out," said Charles Bridgewater, "but I'm going to hang on long enough to see that you get what you deserve, David. I should have turned you over to the police years ago, when I suspected that you were instrumental in the death of your own mother, but instead like a fool, I felt sympathy for you and sent you away instead. That was a horrid mistake—and Daniel paid for my stupid mistake with his life. I can never forgive myself for that." He shook his small fist at David and then buried his head in his hands. Amy rushed over to the man and encircled him in her arms.

"I don't understand," David said, finally, as he realized that his clever plot had come unraveled.

"There were many things you did wrong, David," said Shoop, opening his pocket notebook and going down a list with his finger. "You didn't account for bullet angle, ballistics, including the acoustic profile of a gun shot which told us—or rather told Dr. Barnes here—a lot about just how, how far, and at what angle the gun was shot."

"You also didn't account for the personal side," said Amy, lifting her head from the shoulders of Charles Bridgewater. "I called and called Daniel's phone after Saturday night and he—you—never answered. Daniel would never do that."

"Who are you?" asked David, sneering.

"I'm Daniel's wife," cried Amy, tears staining her cheeks and the shoulder of her father-in-law. She held out her hand and showed him a beautiful diamond ring.

"That's my mother's ring!" exclaimed David.

"No," responded Charles, "It's Amy's ring now. Daniel gave it to her when they were married." He looked up at his reprobate son and said, "David, you may have killed Daniel—my real son—your brother—but Amy is his widow—and she is pregnant with Daniel's child—my grandchild."

"I think what Charles is saying, David," said Vickers to David, "is that the Bridgewater line will go on—Daniel's line will go on. But your line is dead in the water. Detective," he said, turning to Shoop at the door, "here's your man. You and the local police here can fight over who gets first crack at him." Shoop nodded at Vickers, brought out a set of handcuffs and placed them on David's wrists as one of the local police officers read him his rights.

With the excitement over, Pamela and Rocky said goodbye to Amy and her new father-in-law and asked her to let them know when the baby arrived. Vickers walked the couple to the front door and thanked them for all their help. Pamela and Rocky headed home, knowing that Angela and Kent would be thrilled to hear that the man they had chased all over New Orleans had actually been the killer and had been arrested.

"A bittersweet conclusion," said Rocky to his wife.

"Yes," agreed Pamela, "but maybe baby Bridgewater will turn out to be the greatest carpet manufacturer of them all."

Epilogue

Present time--June 21, Sunday

    The Reardon Regional Zoo was not the standard location for a wedding. Today, however, it was decked out in beautiful flowers, ribbons, and satin finery. A pavilion located in the middle of the zoo, with walk paths heading to the different animal locations, served as the venue for the ceremony. A huge trellis marked the location where the actual exchange of vows would take place. White folding chairs were arranged in circular rows in front of the trellis. Seated in these chairs, guests could look around them and see—and hear—in the distance, exotic birds, elephants, camels, giraffes, monkeys, and a variety of smaller creatures. The noise of wedding guests mingled with the cries of exotic fauna made for a truly unique matrimonial experience—or at least that's what Pamela thought as she slid into one of the seats in the second row.
    "I hope they don't call during the ceremony," she said to Rocky who was accompanying her, and who looked dashing in his summer suit—beige with his pale blue shirt and satin blue and beige tie. She was wearing a multi-colored flowery chiffon and a big-brimmed straw hat. She never wore hats, usually, but if you couldn't wear a hat to an outdoor summer wedding, where else?
    "Unlikely," replied her husband, "but, in case, better put your cell on vibrate."
    "I can't do that," she retorted, "I'd just want to answer it then, and I can't during the ceremony."
    "Just how likely is it to happen right during the ceremony? I mean, most weddings only last about twenty

minutes. Ours was longer—it seemed like an eternity before they actually approved us as legal."

"You were just anxious to...."

"I'm always anxious," he said, smiling, his eyebrows wafting up and down in their usual amorous movement.

Shreeech!

"What was that?" she cried.

"Some weird monkey or bird," he said. "It is a zoo, remember."

"I know," she answered, "Can you believe it? A wedding at a zoo! Leave it to Bob and Arliss to think of that."

"What was that?" she cried again.

"I didn't hear anything," he said.

"Oh, it's my cell," she said, pulling her phone from her small formal clutch purse. She looked at the caller ID. "It's Harold." She greeted the lawyer on her cell phone, then listened as he spoke, nodding, smiling, and saying "yes" as he talked. When she hung up, she was excited.

"Amy had a boy—six pounds, eight ounces! Mother and son are doing well. Grandfather Bridgewater is too especially now that he has a new grandson. Not so well physically, but still holding on."

"That's great!" said Rocky, "Oops! Here come your friends." As he spoke, Joan and Willard slipped into the seats beside them. Joan was the epitome of elegance in a a brocade suit and Willard was his jaunty best in crimson and grey seersucker.

"You're just in time," Pamela said, looking at her watch. Indeed, immediately recorded music rang out from the zoo's loudspeaker system. Pamela and the rest turned and watched as Arliss MacGregor, dressed in a simple, yet lovely white tulle gown proceeded down between the rows of seats on the arm of an older gentleman that Pamela surmised was her father. As Pamela looked back at the central trellis, she saw that Bob Goodman had appeared from under the flowered bower, Mitchell Marks at his side as his best man. Arliss glowed as she reached Bob. Bob beamed. Pamela thought happy thoughts and mentally sent best wishes to Amy Bridgewater and her new son and wished them a wonderful life—just as she sent best wishes for a wonderful life to the two wonderful people standing in front of her who were just starting their life together.

An elephant roared. A bird squawked. The lovely sounds of a summer day. Oh, how she loved sounds!

Rocky's Recipes

Pork Roast with Raisin Sauce

4 lb. boneless pork roast
½ tsp. of salt, cinnamon
¼ tsp. of garlic powder, pepper, and cumin

Rub the spices over pork. Roast uncovered until meat thermometer registers 170 degrees (about 2 and ½ hours). Serve with raisin sauce.

Raisin Sauce

1 ½ cup apple juice   1 ½ cup raisins
¼ cup maple syrup   ½ tsp. cinnamon
2 tbsp. cold water   1 tsp. cornstarch

Heat juice, raisins, syrup and cinnamon to boil. Reduce to simmer, add raisins and cook until tender (10 min.) Mix water and cornstarch in small bowl. Add to mixture and bring to boil, stirring (about a minute).

Chocolate Coconut Bars

4 cups crushed graham crackers   1 cup softened butter
½ cup powdered sugar   2 cups shredded coconut
1 can sweetened condensed milk   1 tsp. vanilla
1 cup chopped walnuts   12-oz. bag/ chocolate chips

Preheat oven to 350 degrees. Mix crackers, butter and sugar and pat into bottom of 9' X 13" pan. Bake 10 minutes. Mix coconut, milk, and vanilla. Spread over crust and bake additional 10 minutes. Melt chips in microwave until spreadable. Spread on top of coconut layer. Top with walnuts. Cool and cut into squares.

FM for Murder is the second book in the Pamela Barnes acoustic mystery series. The first, *Sounds of Murder*, represented Patricia Rockwell's debut novel.

Patricia Rockwell has spent most of her life teaching. Her Bachelors' and Masters' degrees are from the University of Nebraska in Speech, and her Ph.D. is from the University of Arizona in Communication. She was on the faculty at the University of Louisiana at Lafayette for thirteen years, retiring in 2007. Her publications are extensive, with over 20 peer-reviewed articles in scholarly journals, several textbooks, and a research volume published by Edwin Mellen Press. In addition, she served for eight years as editor of the *Louisiana Communication Journal*. Her research focuses primarily on deception, sarcasm, and vocal cues. Dr. Rockwell is presently living in Aurora, Illinois, with her husband Milt, also a retired educator. The couple has two adult children.

Made in the USA
Lexington, KY
20 April 2013